'What do you want?' Lucinda breathed.

'I'm not sure,' Rafe said softly. 'Would it sound stupid if I said your approval?'

'*My* approval!' she said. 'And why would you want that? Because you don't like to think that anyone can be immune to your charm?'

'Not at all,' he said calmly. 'I know that you aren't immune to me, Lucinda. You're flesh and blood, aren't you?'

Abigail Gordon began writing some years ago at the suggestion of her sister, who is herself an established writer. She has found it an absorbing and fulfilling way of expressing herself, and feels that in the medical romance there is an opportunity to present realistically strong dramatic situations with which readers can identify. Abigail lives in a Cheshire village near Stockport, and is widowed with three grown-up sons and several grandchildren.

Recent titles by the same author:

OUTLOOK—PROMISING
RESPONDING TO TREATMENT
CRISIS FOR CASSANDRA

PRECIOUS OFFERINGS

BY
ABIGAIL GORDON

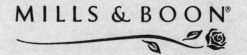

MILLS & BOON®

*MILLS & BOON and MILLS & BOON with the Rose Device
are registered trademarks of the publisher.*

*First published in Great Britain 1998
Harlequin Mills & Boon Limited,
Eton House, 18-24 Paradise Road, Richmond, Surrey TW9 1SR*

© Abigail Gordon 1998

ISBN 0 263 80782 7

*Set in Times 10 on 12 pt. by
Rowland Phototypesetting Limited
Bury St Edmunds, Suffolk*

03-9805-48082-D

*Printed and bound in Great Britain
by Mackays of Chatham PLC, Chatham*

CHAPTER ONE

SEATED in a pew in the village church, Lucinda Beckman shifted uncomfortably as she eyed the smiling group around the font.

A heater on the wall beside her, switched on to take the November chill out of the place, was causing her feet to throb and making her long winter coat of soft rose cashmere feel like a strait-jacket.

Yet her discomfort was mental rather than physical. She was wishing that she hadn't accepted the invitation to attend the Marsland baby's christening.

The child was adorable, her parents ecstatic, but the occasion wasn't the norm for a busy orthopaedic consultant who went in for no strings attached when it came to *her* private life.

This is not my scene, she thought glumly, as she eased her feet out of elegant black shoes. I shouldn't have accepted Cassandra's invitation. For one thing the cold glare that the baby's father had bestowed on her would have been enough to send a lesser mortal scurrying for cover, and, added to that, having to gaze upon the pride and happiness of the two godmothers and their respective husbands, along with that of the bashful teenage godfather, was making her wish herself a thousand miles away.

The vicar's voice came drifting across. 'Name this child,' he commanded, and was duly informed that the tiny scrap was to be called Imogen Barbara.

As the baptismal water splashed upon her brow the

newest member of the Marsland family began to exercise her lungs, and as Bevan Marsland and his wife exchanged smiles Lucinda's eyes were bleak.

She liked Cassandra Marsland, liked her a lot, and her regard would have included Bevan too, if he had let it, but there was a long shadow cast over her relationship with the village's forthright GP, and because of a certain grave in a churchyard not far away she doubted that it would ever lift.

The baptism was over and the cluster of those who had attended were making their way back to the spacious detached house of Cotswold stone where the Marslands lived.

'You'll come back for some food, won't you, Lucinda?' Cassandra coaxed as they came out of the church's gloom into winter sunlight.

That hadn't been her intention, but Lucinda guessed that the ex-senior sister of Springfield Community Hospital was aware of her discomfiture and wanted to dispel it, in spite of her husband's antipathy towards the Infirmary's cool, often abrasive orthopaedic wizard.

And so, because she didn't want to cast any bad vibes over what was a very special day for Cassandra, Lucinda dragged up a smile and questioned, 'Are you sure? I don't want to butt in amongst your family and friends.'

The blonde mother shook her head. 'You're a friend too. At least I like to think you are. . .and that the past is forgotten and forgiven.'

Lucinda's face was sombre as she looked at Bevan's broad back as he walked in front of them. 'You're a generous woman, Cassie. . .but Bevan doesn't feel the same way.'

'He will,' she said confidently, and, gently taking her new daughter from her eldest godmother, she placed the small white bundle in Lucinda's arms.

It was at that moment that a high-powered motorcycle came alongside, swishing to a halt at the curb edge and bringing forth a startled wail from the baby.

Lucinda glared at its helmeted rider. Did he have to make all that racket? But, quite unconcerned, the man was divesting himself of his head-gear and saluting Bevan Marsland, who had turned like the rest of them at the sound of his arrival.

'Rafe!' the village GP cried as a head of dark bronze hair was revealed above a smiling, strong-boned face. 'What are *you* doing here?'

The rest of them were eyeing the man on the bike questioningly. Turning to his wife, Bevan said, 'I can't believe my eyes, Cassie...this is Rafe Davidson...you'll have heard me speak of him. We were out in Bosnia together.'

'Of course!' she cried. 'Welcome to Gloucestershire, Rafe. We've just been christening our brand-new daughter and are now going back for a buffet lunch. Would you care to join us?'

While the conversation was taking place Lucinda was trying to soothe little Imogen, head bent over the baby that she'd been suddenly presented with, and wishing that they would all stop dawdling with this Hell's Angel type so that they could get back to the house and she could unload the infant, as she could feel a damp patch spreading across the sleeve of her beautiful cashmere coat.

When she looked up, feeling much less than her usual cool self, the biker's eyes were on her, and she thought illogically that the deep hazel of them matched his thick bronze locks perfectly.

His glance was only fractional, however. He was reply-
ing to Cassandra's invitation with a smile that would draw
the ducks off the water.

'I'd love to join you, if I may.' He swivelled to face his
friend. 'You perhaps remember that I come from these
parts, Bevan. I've moved back home for a while, and,
recollecting that you'd moved in this direction yourself
after Bosnia, I thought I'd look you up. And lo and behold,
I've already found you.'

Mark, Cassandra's son from a previous relationship and
Imogen's godfather, was eyeing his bike admiringly, and,
observing his interest, the newcomer said, 'Like to come
for a run afterwards? I can't take you on the road, as you're
not old enough, but a nearby field should be OK for a few
quick turns.'

'Sure thing!' the boy said enthusiastically, his shyness
disappearing at the prospect.

This one wasn't short of confidence, Lucinda thought
sourly. He'd no sooner appeared than he was taking over,
but it didn't seem to be bothering Cassandra and Bevan
and she supposed that as she herself was a hanger-on she'd
better mind her own business.

Back at the house Cassie relieved her of the baby, and
as she took off her coat the man called Rafe Davidson said
whimsically in her ear, '*I* won't tell if you won't.'

She eyed him blankly. 'Tell what?'

'That you've dribbled all over your sleeve.'

'You think that's funny?' she asked, keeping a
straight face.

'Yes,' he said, eyeing her approvingly, 'but it's quite
obvious that *you* don't. However, I suppose I shouldn't
joke with people I haven't been introduced to, so shall we
exchange names?'

'I already know yours,' she told him drily. 'Bevan said that you're called Rafe Davidson.'

His eyes were laughing into hers. 'Correct. And we're digressing...you are...?'

'Lucinda Beckman, head of orthopaedics at the Infirmary,' Cassandra's voice said from behind before Lucinda could enlighten him. 'All of us here are part of the medical fraternity, with the exception of Mark and the farmer husband of Joan Jarvis, one of our daughter's godmothers.'

'Joan was previously matron-manager of Springfield Community Hospital, where I was senior sister, and Imogen's other godmother is Gabriella Lassiter, who is a nurse in that same establishment. While her husband, Ethan, the tall, fair haired man at her side, is its new manager. So, Rafe, with regard to what you've just been telling Bevan and I, you will be in good company.'

Lucinda felt her jaw drop. What was that supposed to mean? That Mr Confident was an NHS recruit too? Probably a student, she thought as he pushed back a stray lock of the glinting hair that had fallen onto his brow, although he looked a bit long in the tooth for that.

Cassandra had passed on to her other guests, and as Lucinda eyed him questioningly he said, 'You've heard of the guy who comes into the wards with his little hacksaw to cut off the wedding rings of poor ladies who have injured their hands?'

'Ye-es?' she said warily.

His mouth curved into a puckish smile. 'So have I. Look out for me with my little tool-kit on Monday morning, eh?' And he sauntered off to where young Mark was waiting for him.

*　　*　　*

Driving home, Lucinda went over the last few hours. She'd discovered two things during that time. The first was that, due to Cassandra's sweet reasoning, Bevan's animosity towards herself was lessening.

She didn't think he would ever forgive her for being partly responsible for his brother's death—a circumstance that had left Cassandra pregnant with an illegitimate child, who was now Bevan's stepson as well as his nephew—but ever since meeting up with him Lucinda had hoped that his anger would decrease with the passing years, At last it looked as if there might be a chance.

He'd spoken to her civilly today, for the first time since he'd discovered her complicity in Darren's death, and she was grateful for the crumb he'd thrown her.

It was from that time long ago, and the pain from another fraught happening in her past, that her future had been moulded. The desire to succeed took precedence over everything else because it was the only thing that blotted out remorse and grief, and if folks saw her as a tough female it was because that was what she wanted them to think.

There had been a lot of raised eyebrows when she'd come to the Infirmary as the youngest consultant ever, to take over from Oliver Grant as head of orthopaedics, and because she knew that she was good at the job—brilliant, in fact—Lucinda hadn't hesitated in making her presence felt.

However, before she'd come to the Infirmary there had been one detour as she'd climbed the career ladder. A short period when she'd admitted that there were other things in life besides deformities of the bone and suchlike.

She'd married Piers Beckman, a solicitor, and a man much older than herself, whom she'd treated for a badly fractured leg. It had never been her policy to get involved with patients, but in that instance she had broken the code, letting his protective affection persuade her that he could make her happy while at the same time bringing calm into her life.

It had worked up to a point during their short married life. A registrar in a busy northern hospital at the time, used to throwing herself into bed in adequate lodgings at the end of each busy day, Lucinda had appreciated having someone to come home to in the comfort of Piers' large house, and if the relationship had been low on excitement it had made up for it in security.

They hadn't been married long enough for her to discover if she'd made the right decision. She'd gone home one night to find Piers dead from a massive heart attack. In her grief she had been aware that she mourned him more as a father than a lover, and maybe in that she had her answer.

When she'd stood at the graveside with his son and daughter, who were of a similar age to herself, Lucinda had thought bleakly that it was the end of a short, sweet interlude, that losing those she cared for seemed to be the pattern of her life.

She and her young brother had been left parentless when she was in her late teens, and ever since she'd felt lost and rootless—until Piers had come along.

With him gone the big house had become an empty shell rather than a haven, and soon after his death she had bidden goodbye to his likeable children and made a career move down south.

After a couple of further moves she had ended up in the Midlands, and at the present time was content to remain in the niche at the Infirmary that she was now firmly slotted into.

The second thing that she'd noticed during the christening lunch was that Bevan's friend, newly back from Bosnia, had the sort of magnetism that attracts others, and as she'd made an early departure she had seen that he was keeping the rest of the party enthralled with a string of amusing anecdotes about the things that he and Bevan had got up to in the former Yugoslavia.

There were a couple of things about him that had irritated her. The fact that anyone in their right mind could find anything to laugh about in the carnage out there was one, and the job description that he'd so blithely given her was the other. She could just see the World Health Organisation sending someone out to the war zones to remove jewellery from swollen fingers!

The ultra-modern furnishings of her flat seemed garish and tasteless after the mellow charm of the Marsland house, and as she walked across to the answering machine, kicking off her shoes as she did so, Lucinda thought that her abode was like its owner—expensive and overstated.

Her brother's voice came into the room as she switched on and she tensed. A call from Jake usually meant trouble. At twenty-two years old, he had a lifestyle even more reckless than her own had been at that age, and he seemed to move from one crisis to another.

The one to beat all others had happened almost twelve months ago, when he had gone backpacking in Kashmir and been kidnapped by rebels.

Completely out of her depth for once, Lucinda had flown out to Islamabad along with Ethan Lassiter, the manager of the Springfield Community Hospital, who at that time had been unmarried and had given in to her pleas to go with her for moral support.

They had arrived to discover that, fortunately for him, Jake had been released. Weak with relief, she had stayed on until he'd been given clearance by the authorities, leaving Ethan to fly back to spend Christmas with Gabriella, the beautiful young nurse that he had eventually married.

And now, as her brother said chirpily, 'Hi, Luce, it's me, Jake. Can you get back to me?' she was praying that for once he wasn't going to bring trauma into her life.

But it was a vain hope.

On returning the call, she said, 'Hello, little brother,' in the husky voice that soon became strident when she was angry. 'To what do I owe this honour?'

'I rang to ask how you'd feel about being an auntie,' he said, with just the merest hesitation.

'What do you mean by that?' she asked slowly.

'Melanie's pregnant.'

'Wha-a-at?' she breathed. 'Pregnant! How come?'

'Don't be daft, sis,' he said uneasily. 'You know how come.'

'You...are...completely...irresponsible,' she said in cold anger. 'What about college? You've another twelve months to do and no way are you going to give up now.'

'I don't intend to,' he told her placatingly. '*You'll* help us out until I qualify, won't you, Luce?'

Lucinda sank down onto a black leather chair and eyed the phone glacially. 'Have you two not heard about the pill? That a woman doesn't have to get pregnant these days?'

'Yes, of course we have,' he admitted, with growing discomfort. 'But Melly's doctor wouldn't prescribe it for her because her family have a history of high blood pressure.'

'A possibility of hypertension doesn't have to rule out

other methods of contraception,' Lucinda persisted grimly, aware that although this problem didn't come up to the Kashmir one it wasn't far behind, especially as it would be long term.

But the trouble was there was no way she *could* leave the two youngsters to face it alone. She'd looked after Jake for as long as she could remember. He was the only family she had. The only person she loved utterly and completely.

'We'll have to talk this through, Jake,' she told him in a less angry tone. 'When?'

'One night during the week?' he suggested, with relief in his voice.

Lucinda sighed. Now he'd got it off his chest Jake was feeling better, but he'd unloaded it onto her, as he usually did, and at this moment *she*, felt devastated.

'Yes, I've a free night on Tuesday,' she agreed. 'We'll go out for a meal. . .the three of us.'

'Thanks, Luce,' he said gratefully. 'You'll be proud of me one day. . .I promise.'

'Yes, but will I be able to hold onto my sanity that long?' she said tartly, and replaced the receiver.

As silence descended on the flat once more she went into the bedroom and stripped off. Once the close-fitting black dress and lacy underwear that she'd worn for the christening had been discarded, and the rose cashmere coat placed carefully on its hanger, Lucinda stood in front of the mirror deep in thought.

She wasn't seeing the glossy ebony hair that she'd swept back with silver combs. Or the smooth ivory face with its high cheekbones and dark-lashed eyes. Even the coltish nakedness of her body, with its high pointed breasts and tempting thighs, was wasted on her.

Her mind was darting to and fro between the events of

the christening party and the news that she'd just been given. The images of two children were whirling around in her thoughts: little Imogen and Jake and Melanie's unborn foetus.

What a difference there would be to their start in life, and yet the fact that they had both been conceived in love should mean something, she supposed, as she had no doubts about the depth of the affection between her brother and his girlfriend.

But what did *she* know of such matters? Love was low on the agenda of things that made Lucinda Beckman tick. Success and job satisfaction came high on it because they were food and drink to her. The man hadn't been born who could capture her heart, and she'd met plenty of them in her time.

The clock on her dressing table said seven-thirty and she sighed. There was nowhere she wanted to go and it was too early to go to bed, so it looked as if a book and a dry martini were the answer to another solitary evening.

With the thought of the following day's heavy caseload at the back of her mind, at ten o'clock she turned out the lights and settled down to sleep.

There were depressing grey skies and an equally unacceptable drizzle as Lucinda parked her new Mercedes in its allocated spot in the Infirmary car park the next morning.

The weather matched her mood. Her first thought on waking had been of Jake's unacceptable news of the night before and, fond as she was of him, she'd wished that he would allow her to get on with her own life instead of constantly being dragged into his.

A big BMW motorcycle was parked in the spot that was reserved for the head of the cardiac unit and Lucinda gave a tight smile. It looked as if Bevan Marsland's ebullient friend from yesterday had arrived to take up his duties, whatever they might be. Elderly Sir Thomas Simmons, the top heart man at the Infirmary, wasn't going to be pleased when he found the machine in his parking place. He could be a peppery old blighter when he wanted to be.

As if to give substance to her surmise that Rafe Davidson had arrived, a voice said from behind her, 'We meet again, Lucinda.'

She swung round and there he was, looking just as relaxed and confident as he'd been the previous day and with the same easy smile on his attractive face.

In her present frame of mind it peeved her that he should be feeling so equable while *she* was bogged down with work, and worry about Jake. Letting it show, she said icily, 'Good morning, Mr Davidson. I don't think Sir Thomas is going to be too chuffed when he sees that you've invaded his parking space.'

Unabashed, he grinned back at her. 'Sir Tom and I are old mates.'

'I'll bet!'

'You don't believe me?'

'No, not unless his wife has had her wedding ring stuck on some occasion.'

He raised his eyebrows in assumed surprise. 'Witty as well as wild, I see.'

'Wild?' she gritted. 'From where did you get that titbit?'

'So it's true?'

Her patience was running out. If this stranger had nothing better to do than make light conversation... *she* had.

'You'll have to excuse me,' she said, pushing past him. 'I have a very heavy day ahead.'

He stepped back. 'Of course. Haven't we all?'

Lucinda eyed him dubiously. The first chance she got she would ring Personnel and check up on this fellow, find out what his job was. He'd told Cassandra and Bevan that he was going to be working at the Infirmary, but she would believe it when she saw it.

Her secretary, Monica, a smart, middle-aged woman, and one of the few people who really appreciated the pressures that her clever boss worked under, had picked up an item of gossip from the hospital grapevine and was eager to pass it on when Lucinda arrived at the consultancy suite.

'Guess what, Dr Beckman,' she said, eyes bright with the knowledge that she was about to impart. 'Sir Thomas has got himself a new second-in-command.'

'What?' Lucinda questioned absently as she eyed the pile of paperwork on her desk.

'Sir Thomas has brought in a new guy from London.'

Monica had her attention now. 'Really? I wonder who he is and how good he is. Old Simmons won't have just anybody working for him.'

'That's all I know,' her secretary said, 'but we'll soon find out. His Greatness is bringing him round to meet the other consultants.'

Lucinda sighed. 'There's only Sir Tom who would do the old-style courtesy thing. Doesn't the old guy realise that we've all got a hectic day ahead of us without having to go through the niceties with regard to some big city cardiac boy?'

Something in Monica's expression told her that they weren't alone, and when she swung round her face slackened with amazement. Sir Thomas, in his black coat and pinstriped trousers, was with the man that she'd already met twice in two days—and been irritated by on both occasions.

'Good morning, Dr Beckman,' the elderly consultant said, and, indicating his companion, whose riding leathers appeared to have been concealing a smart tweed suit, he added, 'Allow me to introduce my new colleague, Rafe Davidson.'

At that moment the phone rang and Monica said, 'It's for you, Sir Thomas.'

The old man tutted irritably, 'Excuse me a moment, will you?'

Lucinda said, 'Well, Dr Davidson, I hope that you'll be happy here.'

There was a wicked gleam in his eyes. 'Have you any doubts?'

'Er. . .no. . .' she croaked, with a continuance of the uncharacteristic lack of panache that his arrival had brought about.

When the two men had gone Lucinda slumped into the chair behind her desk and Monica began to laugh. 'What a man!' she giggled. 'The female population will be queue-ing up for heart surgery.'

'I feel as if I'm already heading for a cardiac arrest,' Lucinda told her. 'I was introduced to him yesterday at the Marslands' christening, where he rolled up on a BMW motorcycle. He tried to tell me that his job was cutting wedding rings off swollen fingers, and now I find that he's Sir Thomas's new whizz-kid!'

'There's no doubt about the whizz,' the other woman replied, 'but that man is no kid.'

'No, it would appear not,' Lucinda agreed. 'He was out with the same medical team as Bevan Marsland in Bosnia.'

'Really?'

Her secretary was duly impressed, and Lucinda had to admit that so was she, but she would postpone judgement until she'd seen Rafe Davidson in action. She thought wryly that these days she was more interested in how a man performed in Theatre than how he performed in bed.

But she had some performing to do in Theatre herself this afternoon, plus a heavy clinic this morning, and if she was to get through what she had planned for the day she had better start moving.

The first patient in her Monday morning clinic was a young baby with infantile torticollis, a condition of the neck that had become obvious shortly after birth, due to a muscle being partly fibrous and failing to elongate as the child moved its head.

When Lucinda and her team had first seen the baby a lump in the muscle had already been visible, and she had recommended daily physiotherapy to gently stretch the neck. It had involved moving the head away from the affected area in the direction of the opposite shoulder, and the anxious parents had been instructed to place the infant on alternate sides while sleeping.

In previous instances, where the deformity had been missed in the early stages of life, or the stretching hadn't been successful, she had operated to divide the tendon, usually at its lower level. However, in this instance, after examining the tiny patient, she was able to tell the parents that the physiotherapy was working.

Leaving one of her assistants to accept their delighted expressions of relief, Lucinda moved briskly to the next cubicle—presenting to the onlooker a woman supremely confident of her abilities job-wise, but not so sure about other areas of her life.

And so the morning progressed, for the most part examinations of the stiff, distorted joints of the older population. But amongst them were those of a small girl, whose results from tests taken previously were showing juvenile rhuematoid arthritis—or Still's disease, as it is sometimes known—a very distressing condition in the young.

Jessica Brown had initially had a fever, along with a rash and abdominal pains. Because at that time she had just come back from holidaying abroad, and the stiffness in the joints had been minimal, there had been some delay in the GP sending the child for orthopaedic investigation.

But now, some time after the initial illness, she was experiencing painful swelling of the joints, and Lucinda wasn't looking forward to telling her mother the results of the tests.

Mrs Brown was trying to control a restless toddler as well as comforting Jessica during the interview, and when Lucinda explained carefully what the problem was the mother, already stressed, began to weep uncontrollably.

That in turn upset the children even more, and in the middle of the ensuing bedlam—with Lucinda holding the baby and Monica dashing out to forage for sweets to pacify the children, and find a cup of tea for the stricken mother—the memory of her brother's phone call the previous night came back to Lucinda.

Today *would* have to be all babies and worried mothers, she thought grimly, and those she'd seen weren't penniless students either. How were Jake and Melanie going to manage?

She straightened her shoulders. She'd long since mastered the art of shutting out everything else when she was on the job and today needed to be the same.

When silence was eventually restored she began to

explain to the young mother the treatment that Jessica was going to need, which would include anti-inflammatory drugs. If the disease became more severe than at the present time, she would need splints to relieve acutely inflamed joints during the day.

As the tear-stained little family departed, Lucinda allowed herself a moment's respite. It was no joke for a parent to be given that kind of news, but at least Jessica would get better, as that kind of arthritis in children usually disappeared eventually.

It was the children with gaunt faces and hairless heads whom one saw walking weakly around the Infirmary that one had to grieve for the most. There wasn't always a promise of recovery for them.

Like many others before it, the morning progressed with little time to wonder how the hospital's new 'heart-throb' was settling in on his first day. The infirmary of a Cotswold town would be a far cry from London, that was for sure, and Lucinda wondered what had brought him to her part of the world.

After soup and a roll and a quick cup of tea, Lucinda went to get her car out for a visit to Springfield Community Hospital, where many of her patients were transferred for post-operative care.

Her stay would be brief, as she was in Theatre for most of the afternoon, but she wanted to see for herself how two of last week's surgery cases were progressing.

The motorcycle was still there, its splendour over-shadowed by Sir Thomas's sleek Jaguar, and as she eyed it Rafe Davidson appeared, striding easily towards her.

His quirky smile flashed out and she responded with a restrained effort of her own.

'Hi,' he said. 'Where are you off to?'

On a really bad day she would have told him to mind his own business, but with food inside her, and the November sun warmer than of late, her spirits were lifting, and so she answered obligingly, 'I'm going to Springfield to check on a couple of my patients.'

'Ah, and where might that be?'

She pointed vaguely in a northerly direction and he said immediately, 'I'm going that way. Want a lift?'

Lucinda stared at him. This guy's manner was so easy she'd like to bet that he had folks eating out of his hand wherever he went. She'd met doctors like him before, who laughed and joked their way through the never-ending maze of health problems.

Well, nobody knew better than she that illness was no laughing matter, and he had another think coming if he thought he could enslave the uncharmable Dr Beckman. But before sending him on his way she wanted to know what he had in mind. . .just to satisfy her curiosity.

'I don't need a lift,' she pointed out coolly. 'I came by car.'

'Yes, I've duly noted the Merc,' he said. 'But it's much quicker on the bike, especially as you're going in your lunch-hour.

'How do you know it's my lunch-hour?'

'Simple. I saw you gulping down the food in the restaurant as if your next moment would be your last.'

'So you were watching me!'

'Any reason why not? There are things that I've enjoyed watching a lot less.'

'Have you ever been put down?' she said coldly. 'Or are you always as pushy as this?'

He threw back his head and laughed, showing strong white teeth. 'I'm not sure what you mean by "put down", but, yes, I have been "put down" many a time. . .in many ways. And now that we've established that, are you going to let me give you a lift?'

A sudden vision of zooming along the road on his powerful bike, with the wind in her face and his broad back to hold onto, came into her mind, and because she was wearing flat shoes and trousers, with a warm suede jacket, she weakened.

'All right, yes. I certainly have a busy day ahead of me and time is of the essence. But what about a helmet?'

He stretched out his hands, palms upwards, and shrugged. 'Everything to hand, madam,' he said, and, bending, opened one of the side panniers and produced a helmet.

When she'd settled herself behind him, he turned and gave her a quick glance before they set off. 'You can hold onto me as tightly as you like,' he offered.

'I prefer to grip the seat instead,' she told him straight-faced. 'That way I'm not likely to come to grief.' As amusement glinted in the most disturbing eyes she'd ever seen, Lucinda hoped that he'd got the message.

CHAPTER TWO

As LUCINDA got off the back of the bike at the entrance to Springfield, Rafe Davidson said, 'How long will you be? I'll collect you on my way back.'

'Three quarters of an hour,' she said briefly, wishing she hadn't allowed herself to be indebted to him for the return journey.

He checked his watch. 'I'll pick you up at one forty-five, then.' And, with the smile that she was beginning to feel mesmerised by, he added, 'See you later, Lucinda.'

She nodded, having no intention of becoming involved in first-name terms on her part. As he revved up the bike, she went quickly into the cottage-type hospital that played its own small but very vital part in the health care of the area.

As she went down its main corridor, Mike Drew, one of the GPs who attended the patients there, was coming towards her, and when he saw her he stopped.

'Hello, there, Lucinda,' he said cheerfully. 'How are you?

'Fine, Mike,' she told him briskly, 'and I don't need to ask how you are. I believe that congratulations are in order.'

'Yes,' he beamed. 'Felice and I were married a fortnight ago. Rachel and Nicholas flew over from America to be with us.'

'I imagine that you're missing Rachel. She was the ideal partner for your practice, wasn't she?' she commented.

'Yes, indeed,' he agreed with a smile. 'But Nicholas

24

also thought she would be the ideal wife, and he and Felice are very persuasive people.'

'Brother and sister hijacking the two local GPs, you mean?'

'Something like that.'

'I'm afraid I must get on,' she told him. 'I've come to check on my patients and was given a lift on the motorcycle of the new cardiac man who has joined the staff at the Infirmary. He's picking me up at a quarter to two.'

Mike was interested to hear about the newcomer and wouldn't let her go until he'd got the name and particulars of Rafe Davidson. 'I've heard a rumour that Sir Thomas is retiring. Is this fellow going to be his replacement, do you think?' he asked as she hovered on one foot, ready to make a getaway.

His question slowed her down. Surely this Rafe Davidson fellow wasn't that good! 'It's the first I've heard of it,' she told him, 'but if that is so, the hospital grapevine will spit the information out before long. You can bet on it.'

The first of the two patients that she'd come to see was a stoical elderly lady with peripheral neuritis, an inflammation of the outer nerves, who had been given a knee replacement.

Under normal circumstances the operation would have been routine, but the fact that the neuritis had taken away all feeling in the leg made it tricky when it came to learning to walk with the new joint.

Although Lucinda had done her part of the surgery with her usual skill, she was afraid that the success of it would be blighted by the neuritis, and she was anxious to see just how well the old lady was walking.

Lucinda discovered that she wasn't doing very well at all, and as the raven-haired doctor eyed the old lady's uneven progress down the ward visions of a knee brace came reluctantly to mind.

The physiotherapist confirmed Lucinda's misgivings, but as she made her way to the general ward to see the second patient she consoled herself that at least the diseased knee had gone.

Marion Wain, a forty-year-old housewife, had been given an autograft three weeks previously. Lucinda had used bone from the top of her hips, known as the iliac crests, to fill the cavity in a diseased bone in her leg. Isobel Graham, who had replaced Cassandra as senior sister at Springfield when she became pregnant, was able to report that X-rays showed the cavity to be filling up satisfactorily.

Some you win, some you lose, Lucinda thought philosophically as she went out onto the hospital forecourt ready for her lift back.

Rafe Davidson was already there, sitting astride the bike, with his helmet in the crook of his arm and the winter sun glinting on the thick bronze of his hair.

'Why didn't you come inside to look round?' she asked abruptly, determined to ignore the fact that he made a striking picture on the powerful machine. 'You'll be coming here frequently to check on your patients.'

'Some other time maybe,' he said absently, and she bridled.

She was right about him. He was going to have to do better than this if he wanted to be counted amongst *her* acquaintances. New brooms were usually desperate to sweep clean, but this one gave the impression that he'd rather push things under the carpet.

Her mouth twisted. She did well to talk about her 'acquaintances'. That was all she could boast of. . .acquaintances. She had no close friends. Probably because people found her intimidating,

That she might be, but she was just, too. No one had ever been able to accuse her of being unfair. Those on the staff of the Infirmary who didn't know her very well walked carefully when she was around, but when they got to know her they showed her respect.

Women usually clung onto their husbands whenever she made one of her rare social appearances, and she'd almost been tempted to put a piece in the paper saying that the men of the parish were quite safe. . .that she wasn't a white witch or a seductress, and that most of the time she was too tired to play those sort of games.

Maybe it was her dark attraction that worried them. Yet they didn't run a mile when they needed a new joint, did they? Or a bone graft, or when they'd slipped a disc. . .

Did any of them know that the word 'orthopaedic' meant a straight child? she thought, as her mind continued to race. That was what she strove to do. . .make sick children—and adults—straight and healthy.

'I've just been to see a patient,' he said with sudden seriousness, as if he sensed her disapproval.

That brought her back into focus. 'I'm not with you. On your first day? Surely not.'

'My parents' home isn't far from here. That's where I'm living at the moment. I took the appointment at the Infirmary to be near them.'

Light was dawning. 'And who is the patient?' she asked carefully, curiosity making her forget that she was supposed to be keeping him at arm's length.

'My mother.'

Lucinda glanced at him from beneath dark lashes. 'I see. And may I ask what's wrong?'

'She was suffering from lack of my company,' he said obliquely as he fastened the strap of his helmet. 'And if *you* are going to get back in time for Theatre, and *I* am going to prevent Sir Tom from sending out a search party for me, we'd better get moving.'

'Thanks for the lift,' she told him as they dismounted from the bike in the Infirmary car park. 'And now I must scoot. My theatre team will be getting scrubbed up.'

Rafe Davidson nodded, but there was no urgency in *him*. 'I'm off the hook, so to speak, with it being my first day. I'm merely absorbing and observing, but no doubt tomorrow. . .'

He mopped his brow in mock fatigue and Lucinda thought that he should have gone on the stage. The acting greats wouldn't have stood a chance.

'What are your first impressions?' she asked, prepared to hang on for another few seconds in the hope of getting a sensible answer to a question this time.

The dark hazel eyes had amusement in them. 'Of what?'

'The Infirmary, of course!' she snapped.

'Building. . .prehistoric,' he said laconically. 'Equipment. . .quite impressive. Staff. . .those I've met so far. . .intriguing. Especially a certain orthopaedic practician who thinks that everybody's out of step except herself.'

If she *had* been warming to the newcomer that would have put the chill on it. He had some cheek! The guy hadn't been in the place five minutes and he'd got her down as a big-head.

'It's not taken you long to tune in to hospital tittle-tattle,' she said coldly. 'The person who said that has two left feet, no doubt. Judge me when you've seen me perform,

Rafe Davidson. In the meantime, I shall no doubt be hearing from similar sources just how handy *you* are when you're called upon to use your "tools".'

'No need to get all steamed up, Lucinda. It's bad for the heart,' he told her with irritating patronage. 'I don't doubt for one moment that you are superb. . .at the job.'

She hunched her shoulders in the suede jacket and took her briefcase out of the pannier of the bike. 'Thanks for the vote of confidence,' she said tightly.

With a strong feeling that Rafe Davidson had sized her up already, she walked quickly towards the Infirmary's main entrance, vowing as she did so that she would give that man a wide berth in future.

An easy enough thing to do for the rest of that day, but there were other days and weeks to follow, and it was inevitable that their paths should cross in the corridors, on the wards, in the car park or the restaurant. Wherever she went Rafe Davidson seemed to be there, smiling his quirky smile and charming everyone except herself.

Maybe it was the extent of his charisma that was making her behave so perversely, she kept thinking, or perhaps it was because he'd settled into the job so quickly—unlike herself when she'd first joined the staff.

She could still remember Bevan Marsland taking her to the dinner dance arranged by the Friends of Springfield Hospital, because they had both been new to the area and neither had had a partner.

It had been shortly after Piers died, when she'd been looking for comfort, and that night had been no different.

In a slightly hysterical state she had realised that she'd met Cassandra before. She had blurted out in front of Bevan that his reckless young brother had made Cassie pregnant all those years ago, when they were students, and that her teenage son, Mark, was his brother's child.

Lucinda had thought that the astonished GP would explode when he'd discovered that Mark was his nephew and Cassie hadn't told him. He was in love with her and hadn't been able to understand why she had kept it from him. Fortunately, it had all come right in the end, and now they were married and had presented Mark with a small sister.

But Bevan had never forgiven Lucinda for the part she'd played in the foolishness that had led to Darren's death, especially as she hadn't owned up to it at the time.

They'd been to a party and had been tipsy. On the way home, Lucinda, who had recently replaced Cassandra in the fickle youth's affections, had dared Darren to climb the church steeple.

Always reckless, he'd accepted the challenge, but had slipped and fallen to his death, leaving her to face a lifetime of remorse and the brunt of Bevan's anger.

She often asked herself why she'd stayed in the area after the tragic past had been brought out of wraps, and she always came up with the same answer. . .better the devil one knows.

Her meeting with Jake and Melanie had been more amicable than she'd intended. Perhaps because they were so much in love and yet shamefully contrite about the unplanned pregnancy.

'I know you must think us stupid, Lucinda, letting it happen when we've no money and nowhere to live,' Melanie had said guiltily, 'but we're both going to get jobs, as well as keeping on with our studies, so that nearer to the time when the baby is due we'll be able to afford a flat. In the meantime, we've still got our rooms in the halls of residence.'

Lucinda had eyed the earnest young face framed by straight blonde hair, and the golden-lashed blue eyes that were having a job to meet her own, and had known that whatever mess they might have got themselves into, this girl was right for the irresponsible Jake.

Darren Marsland had been irresponsible too, all that time ago, but he'd been a conceited flirt as well, and she couldn't say that about Jake. From the moment of their meeting he'd had eyes for no one but his 'Melly'.

Yet she did wish they'd acted more wisely. *She* always looked before she leapt these days. No crazy capers for Dr Beckman, though she'd been anything but prudent when she was their age. It had been with the memory of that in mind that she'd said reasonably, 'The most important thing is to see that you and the baby are all right, Melanie. We'll worry about finances when you're further into the pregnancy. Obviously I'll help financially, but how are you going to complete your degree course with a young baby to care for? That's what I want to know. You have no relatives close by and time is the one thing that is in short supply in my life. My days are long and arduous and. . .'

'We know that, Luce,' Jake had said, without his usual nonchalance. 'Just as long as you'll be there for us, eh, Melly?'

The girl had nodded in mute agreement.

Observing the pair of them, Lucinda had refrained from saying, When have I ever *not* been there for you, Jake?

When the meal had been over the two young ones had gone to a students' meeting and she had walked the short distance back to her flat, feeling low and dispirited.

She hadn't been sure why. The obvious reason was the

pregnancy, but deep inside she had known it wasn't that. Could it be because she envied them their adoration of each other? The love that was so obvious?

It might be that, because *she'd* never felt like that for someone of the opposite sex in the whole of her life. She'd always consoled herself that one didn't miss what one hadn't had, but for once the thought had brought no comfort.

The memory of a pair of quizzical hazel eyes had come into her mind at that moment and she'd wondered if the Infirmary's latest acquisition on the cardiac unit was ever miserable. Or was he just a surface person, all crust and no meat?

A hint that the meat *was* there came on a day when the two cardiac surgeons appeared in the staff restaurant at the same time as herself. As Lucinda was about to seat herself at an empty table Sir Thomas Simmons appeared beside her and announced majestically, 'I thought that we might join you, my dear.'

'Yes, of course,' she said smoothly, aware that Rafe Davidson was only a step behind him and that he was taking in every detail of her smart tailored suit with its matching silk blouse.

'You're looking very swish, Dr Beckman,' he said as he unloaded his tray.

'I've given myself the afternoon off,' she told him. 'One of the sisters on my unit has been off sick for quite some time, and after doing some shopping I'm going to call and see her.'

Thomas Simmons's head had been bent over his plate as he tucked into his meal, but he looked up at that point and remarked, 'I would presume that you're referring to Anne Tavistock?'

'Yes,' she agreed. 'I believe that she saw one of you on the cardiac unit last week and was told that she needs a heart transplant?'

'That is so,' the elderly surgeon said ponderously. 'I saw her myself.'

'It's possible that the transplant may not be necessary, sir,' his companion said.

The other man cleared his throat irritably. 'Not again, Dr Davidson! You know my opinion about treating patients like guinea pigs.'

Rafe Davidson was smiling his enigmatic smile, but it wasn't reaching his eyes. 'The technique has been tried and tested with excellent results,' he argued calmly. 'I'm only sorry that this hospital wasn't chosen to be one of the two in this country where the operation will be performed.'

Lucinda's eyes widened. Nobody, but nobody argued with Sir Thomas. His word was law in the cardiac unit, even though there were those who thought him old-fashioned and pedantic, but this guy wasn't just thinking it, he was spelling it out.

At that moment her interest as a member of the medical profession was uppermost. She put to the back of her mind the fact that every time she saw Rafe Davidson he impinged upon her consciousness so much that whenever she had a minute to spare—and even when she hadn't—she found herself doodling his name. . .his face. . .his body. . .

As if knowing that he had completely captured her attention, he went on to explain, 'You might have read about the new technique for treating cardiac failure, Lucinda. It's called heart shrink surgery and is an alternative to transplants, which are horrendously expensive and not always successful.'

'And *this* is?' his older colleague asked with an angry snort.

'Not always,' Rafe Davidson admitted coolly. 'But the doctors who have been using it have been getting good results. . .and the cost of such surgery is fractional in comparison to what it costs to give a patient a new heart.'

'Uncharted territory!' the other man growled.

'In some ways, yes, but it works. They've proved that. . . and the treatment could revolutionise heart surgery,' he argued, unabashed.

There was a light in his eyes that she'd sometimes seen in her own. It came from the excitement of realising that a cure, or a degree of relief, had been discovered for some grievous ill. An occasion when medical research walked hand in hand with God.

'I've read about it briefly, but what exactly does it entail, Rafe?' she asked, using his first name as naturally as he'd used her own, and barely aware of it because they were on common ground.

'The surgery, entitled left ventricle volume reduction, is self-explanatory to the likes of ourselves,' he replied, 'but basically to cardiac sufferers it means that a diseased, dilated heart will pump much more efficiently when its volume has been reduced. Healthy tissue is removed from the still beating heart while the blood supply is diverted outside the body, and once that has been done the heart is sewn back together.'

Taking his eyes from her own bright gaze, he directed his attention to a glowering Sir Thomas and said levelly, 'And, given the chance, I'd be prepared to try it.'

'You should have stayed at your big London hospital, then,' the other man snapped.

As Lucinda watched she saw Rafe Davidson's face become still, and for the first time since she'd known him he wasn't smiling. 'Or gone to Bristol where a lot of the activity regarding heart shrink surgery has been taking place?' he said quietly. 'But you perhaps recall that I had a very good reason for moving back to my home town.'

Thomas Simmons cleared his throat uncomfortably and for a second Lucinda was sorry for the old martinet. Change didn't come easily to the elderly, especially when one was as revered as he, but surely he saw that Rafe was right? Risks had to be taken sometimes to move medicine along, and if he was more concerned about his reputation than the welfare of those who came to him for help, then it was time for him to hang up his stethoscope.

During the exchange of words between the two men she had only spoken the once. When Sir Thomas got to his feet and said huffily, 'If you'll excuse me, Lucinda, I have a phone call to make,' she found her voice.

'Of course, Sir Thomas.'

When he had gone Rafe Davidson eyed her quizzically and asked, 'And what did our Dr Beckman think of that little slanging match?'

Lucinda's dark eyes were thoughtful. 'I thought that you were right in everything you said, but old Tom Simmons *is* the head of cardiac surgery here, and, as such, is entitled to have his say. However, if you are going to take over from him in the near future then you can change things if you want to, can't you?'

'And what gave you that idea?' he asked curiously.

'What?'

'That Sir Tom is going to retire?

'Er. . .I don't recall. . .' she told him warily. 'Why, isn't that the case?'

'Not at present. I've moved up here for personal reasons.'

'I see. Am I allowed to ask what they are?'

He shrugged. 'It's no secret. I came back to these parts to be near a very special woman.'

She turned her head away so that he wouldn't see the dismay on her face, and yet why should she be dismayed? Rafe Davidson was attractive, a charmer, and obviously intelligent, or he wouldn't be near the top of his field in cardiac surgery. It went without saying that there would already be a woman in his life.

Wasn't that always the case, though? For the first time since he'd pulled his bike up beside her on the day of the christening she'd been feeling an affinity with him, admitting to herself that she wasn't totally unaffected by him. They'd been in tune, even though it was on a job satisfaction level rather than personal. And now here he was, shattering the brief rapport between them by saying that he'd moved from a top London hospital to be near some woman. It wasn't something that she wanted to hear, she thought glumly.

Whoever the woman was, she must have some pull to bring him so far out of London, she thought. With a strange gnawing feeling of having missed the boat, she said tightly, 'I see. So your dedication to cardiac surgery wasn't so strong that you weren't prepared to come to a less prestigious part of the country to continue your employment?'

'Correct,' he agreed blandly. 'I would go to the ends of the earth for her.'

Lucinda felt her throat close up. Was there no end to the stream of lovers who passed before her eyes? Cassandra and Bevan, Gabriella and Ethan Lassiter, the Jarvis couple who'd found love in middle age, Jake and his Melanie... and now, to put the lid on it, the hospital romeo was professing undying love for some female. For an obscure reason that she didn't want to bring out of the shadows, it was the knowledge of Rafe's relationship that she found the most upsetting.

She got to her feet, pushing away her half-eaten meal, and surprisingly he did likewise.

'What have I said now?' he asked, eyeing the set of her shoulders and the grim mouth.

'Nothing. Nothing at all. Like Sir Thomas, if you'll excuse me, I have a phone call to make.' She hadn't, but the excuse would do while she got control of her emotions.

There was puzzlement in his eyes, but he didn't try to stop her. As she went back to her office she was wishing that Rafe Davidson would return to London and take his unknown beloved with him.

But she hadn't seen the last of him. Monica was still at lunch and she had the place to herself, but only for a second. Before she could close the door behind her he was there, and Lucinda felt the colour flood up into her face.

'What do you want?' she breathed.

'I'm not sure,' he said softly. 'Would it sound stupid if I said your approval?'

'*My* approval!' she said. 'And why would you want that? Because you don't like to think anyone can be immune to your charm?'

'Not at all,' he said calmly. 'I know that you aren't immune to me, Lucinda. You're flesh and blood, aren't you?'

'You have some conceit,' she said angrily, putting the

width of her desk between them. 'The only time you come into *my* orbit is job-wise.'

'Is that so?'

He was circling the desk and she thought furiously that he'd read her thoughts out there in the restaurant. He knew that she was beginning to thaw towards him.

As if to give truth to the conjecture; he put his arms around her and, as she stood stiff and unyielding, kissed her gently on the lips.

At the brief caress she wrenched her head away, but, gripping her chin, he swivelled her face back towards him and said in a low voice, 'Don't pretend that you don't want me to kiss you, Lucinda, because you do. And I'm just as willing to warm up the block of ice that you call your heart.'

She pushed him away from her so hard that he almost overbalanced. 'What is it with you?' she panted. 'Only seconds ago you were telling me about the love of your life, but it's not stopping you from a bit of dallying on the way, is it? If you've been told that I'm the hard woman on the staff of the Infirmary, you can believe it. Please don't set out to prove them wrong because you'll be wasting your time.'

His face had closed up. 'The woman I told you about is my mother.'

'Your mother!' she echoed. 'Is she elderly and infirm or something?'

'Far from it.'

'She lives alone, then?'

His easy smile was back. 'Anything but. There's my father, my sister, Zoe, and my younger brother, Miles, at home.'

Lucinda eyed him in bewilderment. She was beginning to tire of this oblique conversation. Monica would be back any moment and they were getting nowhere. But did that matter? Did she *want* to know what made him tick? What motivated the charmer forever at her elbow?

Maybe she'd been right to think this guy was all crust and no meat. What was a man of his age and stature hankering to be back with his mother for? Especially when the nest was far from empty.

She'd coped without both parents and it hadn't always been easy, but it had made her self-reliant. Although, unfortunately, the ability to sort out one's own affairs hadn't rubbed off onto Jake.

As their glances locked she was irritated to discover that her heart was answering the questions she was putting to herself. She *did* want to know what made him tick. She wanted to know everything there was to know about Rafe Davidson. If she should end up being disappointed, it wouldn't be the first time that a member of the male population hadn't come up to scratch as far as she was concerned.

'So, now that you've satisfied yourself that my motives are honourable, shall we carry on where we left off?' he said as his melting brown gaze swept over her vivid face and the ivory column of her throat.

Lucinda's lips parted and she gave a low, reckless laugh. 'Why not? I can fit you in before my first appointment.'

'And I suppose I should be honoured at that offer?'

They were cat-and-mousing. She knew it and so did he, but the challenge had been made and she was waiting to see what he was going to do about it.

He reached out as if to straighten the papers on her desk, but his hand went past them and gripped her wrist, and as he moved towards her the piece of ice that was her heart began to warm up.

This time his kiss wasn't gentle, and yet it wasn't rough. It was an exercise in slow passion, taking her into uncharted seas that were foreign to her. There was tenderness in it, desire, and sheer sexual excitement, and for once she wasn't in charge. This casual, charismatic man was making her feel drowsy and compliant and in that moment nothing else existed but the two of them.

It could have gone on for ever, but in the midst of it Lucinda heard Monica's heels clattering on the tiles of the passage outside. Like someone drunk with heady wine, she said in a slurred whisper, 'My secretary's coming back.'

Rafe Davidson's arms dropped away from her at that, and he freed her lips with a reluctance that brought the fire inside her to fever pitch, making her want to cry out for her secretary to go away.

But, unaware of the passions behind the closed door, Monica knocked briefly. When Lucinda called weakly for her to enter, Monica indicated the armful of files that she was carrying and reminded Lucinda, 'You said that you would dictate the correspondence you want sending out on these cases before you go off for the afternoon, Dr Beckman.'

'Yes, of course,' she agreed mechanically, and, with her eyes still brilliant from the resurrection of the long-dead feelings that the man at her side had just brought to life, added, 'Dr Davidson and I have concluded our business for the time being.'

CHAPTER THREE

SHE'D let the 'Laughing Cavalier' bridge her defences, Lucinda thought as she drove home in the dark November night after visiting the sick nurse. *She*, who had always been attracted to the smouldering types on the occasions when she'd let herself off the hook.

There was certainly nothing smouldering about Rafe Davidson. He was like a lazy river of clear, untroubled water that became a whirlpool when it came up against a rock. He must be laughing fit to burst at the way the 'hard woman' of the Infirmary had collapsed into his arms like a pricked balloon.

Maybe he'd seen *her* as a rock, solid and immovable, and had decided to turn her into molten lava for the fun of it. But he wasn't to know that it had been dismay at hearing about the woman he'd described so lovingly that had caused her brief capitulation. By the time she'd discovered that his 'dearly beloved' was his mother, the degree of consciousness that he evoked in her had taken over her senses.

She was puzzled by his attitude with regard to his mother, especially as he'd assured Lucinda that she wasn't elderly or infirm. Lots of men had a deep affection for their mothers, but they didn't usually voice it as freely as he. *Or* move back home into the family environment without a good reason, after having established themselves in a London hospital.

However, all of that was not her business, but those

41

incredible few moments in her office were. By the time the smart block of flats where she lived came into view, common sense had reared its head and told her that she, of all people, should know that a passionate kiss didn't have to have anything to do with commitment.

Anne Tavistock had been a shadow of her usual energetic self when Lucinda had got there, and Lucinda had been amazed to find that her heart had deteriorated so much in such a short a time.

The sight of Anne had brought Rafe to mind again, along with the memory of his support of the new heart shrink surgery. As she'd watched the pale-faced woman fighting what she described as 'continual exhaustion', Lucinda had known that if the new technique ever became standard, the lives of thousands would benefit from it.

There wouldn't be a lifetime on anti-rejection drugs for them, and recovery from the surgery would be much quicker than after a transplant, but there was no way she was going to raise any false hopes for Anne. It would be cruel to bring hope if there wasn't any and, added to that, each consultant was always loath to interfere with the patients of another, unless asked to do so,

But she vowed that she would mention Anne's condition to Rafe and see what he came up with. After all, Anne was. . .or had been. . .one of her own team, and it was the least she could do.

After garaging her car Lucinda hurried inside, hugging her coat around her as the chill of the night wind nipped her face and ankles. A cosy evening in front of the fire was a tempting thought, and she pulled a wry face at the way her mind worked these days.

At one time she would have been out, no matter what the weather was like, roistering around the bars and clubs and generally living it up with the gang that she went around with. But in her present busy yet solitary life all that seemed an eternity ago, and, of course, it was.

A lot of folks would stare if they knew how very quietly the forceful head of orthopaedics lived. All glitz and glamour on the outside, but inside...what? A mixture of loneliness and supreme confidence...of intolerance and understanding...frigidity that craved passion?

It's no wonder people don't understand you, she told herself as she hurried through revolving doors into the luxurious entrance hall of the flats. You don't even understand yourself.

He was sitting on the cream leather chesterfield with an expensive potted palm on either side of him, while the elderly porter who guarded the privacy of the building and its occupants chatted to him from behind the desk.

Lucinda had stopped in mid-stride at the sight of him, with surprise in her dark eyes and quick pleasure coursing through her, but there was an instant watchfulness there, too, and her greeting was hardly effusive.

'How did you know where I lived?' she asked coolly.

He gave an easy smile. 'Simple. It appears that almost everyone at the Infirmary is aware that Dr Beckman lives in the poshest flats in the area. In fact, from what I've been hearing, your lifestyle is bordering on regal, which makes me hesitate to explain my reason for being here.'

'But nevertheless you are going to?' she commented drily as she unbuttoned her coat to reveal once again the smart suit beneath it. 'Perhaps you'd like to come up to the flat and tell me what this is all about.'

'Yes, of course. I can't think of anything I'd like

better than to see you in your natural habitat.'

Lucinda was pressing the button to summon the lift, and, glancing over her shoulder, she informed him in the same cool manner, 'I don't think I have a natural habitat. I'm something of a cuckoo, and that's an opinion shared by quite a few of the worthy matrons of this parish.'

'What? They're afraid that you're going to land in *their* nests? I've always been under the impression that it takes two to get up to that sort of thing.'

'I suppose there's such a thing as mental adultery,' she said wryly as the lift doors glided open, 'which can be just as upsetting as the real thing. A sultry-looking brunette is looked upon with as much suspicion as the fluffy blonde.'

'You're something of a cynic, aren't you?' he asked, his face straight for once, as they ascended upwards inside the confined space.

'In some ways, yes,' she admitted. 'We surgeons see a lot of the sad and seamy side of life.'

Rafe was frowning. 'Oh, come off it, Lucinda! Medicine is the one thing that will never make a cynic of us. The power to heal brings with it excitement, humility, and a hell of a lot of satisfaction. . .but never cynicism. If that's how you are, it must come from within.'

'All right! So it comes from within!' she snapped, as she put her key in the lock. 'If you've quite finished pointing out my faults, maybe you'll say what you have to say. . .and go.'

'Not until I've seen inside your salubrious abode,' he said calmly. 'You *did* invite me up.

'Wowee!' he exclaimed as the door swung back and he stepped inside. 'You're really into black and chrome! This is very space-ageish.'

'It suits *me*,' she said stiffly, still smarting at his earlier remark.

'Beam me up, Scottie,' he murmured, as if she hadn't spoken.

'I'm tired,' she told him coldly, 'so if you'll just get to the point?'

He swivelled and faced her. 'You say you're tired? Too tired to come out to supper with me?'

'Are you serious?' she asked slowly, with the feeling that one never knew what was coming next with this guy.

'Yes, for once.'

Her spirits lifted, and as if her earlier coolness had never been she asked, 'Where would we be going?'

The vision of a quiet meal in a select restaurant with good wines and delicious food hovered in front of her eyes like an oasis in the desert of a cold winter evening.

'Rowan House,' he replied.

'Is that new? I don't recall having heard of a restaurant of that name.'

'It isn't a restaurant.'

'What is it, then?' she asked carefully, as the dream faded. It would be just like him to take her to a soup kitchen in the town centre, or a transport café where burly men ate bangers and mash and slurped hot tea out of thick mugs.

'You'll have to wait and see. . .that is, if you're coming.'

She started to put her coat back on. 'I'm coming, if only out of curiosity.' Then, with her arm halfway up the sleeve, she asked, 'Am I dressed right for where we're going?' A thought struck her. 'I sincerely hope that you're not on the bike.'

He shook his head. 'No, I've borrowed a car, and as to your outfit. . .you'll do. If the need should arise I can always find you a hard hat and a boiler suit.'

Lucinda glared at him. Some invitation this was turning out to be. But if he thought he was going to throw her off balance now that she'd accepted he had another think coming. Surely in the short time that they'd known each other Rafe Davidson would have sussed out that she was particular where she went, and with whom.

In the close confines of a maroon Rover she could smell the tang of his aftershave, and was near enough to observe the springing russet hair that lay thickly behind his ears. His hands on the steering wheel were relaxed yet steady, and as she breathed in the clean, masculine aura of him her awareness of it sent her thoughts winging back to those moments in her office earlier in the day.

They must have been in his mind too, as his eyes left the road for a second and rested on her face. 'Any regrets, Lucinda?' he asked softly.

'What about?' she hedged.

'Our previous encounter in your office.'

If she were to answer the question truthfully it would be 'no'. But did she want him to think that he only needed to crook his finger and she was ready and willing? Definitely not, and so she told him, 'I never regret having a few moments' flirtation with an attractive man, but that is all. *She* "travels fastest who travels alone".'

She knew that she'd got to him by the look on his face. It wasn't anger that she saw there, or pique. It was difficult to describe his expression. 'Disappointed' was a word that came to mind, but why should that apply?

She'd never pretended to be what she wasn't. Up to now she *had* preferred to travel alone, and, because she wasn't a clinging vine, most of the time she'd been left to get on with it.

But that had been before she'd met a man who kissed like an angel, smiled most of the time, had no malice in him and was very fanciable into the bargain. With a quakey feeling in the pit of her stomach, she was wishing that she hadn't been so flippant and dismissive when she'd answered his question.

There wasn't time to do anything about it, though. The car had left the road that led out of the town and was pulling up outside a large house in spacious grounds.

'Rowan House Hospice' it said on a board just inside large wrought-iron gates, and Lucinda turned to him in puzzlement. This wasn't a soup kitchen or a transport café, but it was just as unexpected a place to be arriving at.

For a second irritation swamped her curiosity. Just for once she'd have liked to get away from the NHS, with its sick and suffering. Eyeing her expression, he said slowly, 'I suppose you think I've brought you here under false pretences.'

'I don't know what I think,' she told him truthfully, 'but I would have liked to get away from healthcare for a few hours.'

He pursed his lips. 'I must confess that side of it didn't occur to me when I invited you, but I do assure you that the invitation is genuine enough.' She listened expectantly as he went on with a wealth of sadness in his voice, 'I *am* taking you to a supper party. Not a last supper, although I'm afraid that will come soon enough, but a get-together for my family on the occasion of my mother's birthday.'

Lucinda felt her mouth go dry. 'Your mother is in here?' she breathed.

'I'm afraid so. She has terminal cancer and hasn't long to live.'

Her mind was reeling. 'So that's why you came back to

this part of the country...to be near her?' And to think that she'd had him down as tied to his mother's apron strings, she thought shamefully.

When he spoke again his voice was low and very sad. 'Yes. She'd had cancer previously, but had been told it was cured. When it came back she wouldn't let my father tell me at first...didn't want to worry me...otherwise I would have been back long ago. That's the way she's always been...putting Dad and the rest of us first, even at a time like this.'

Lucinda's sympathy was mingled with embarrassment as she said uncomfortably, 'Surely your mother won't want a stranger at her party? I shall feel as if I'm intruding.'

Rafe smiled for the first time since they'd arrived at the hospice. 'You don't know my family. My mum has always made all our friends welcome. Our house is always full. She loves people.'

'Yes, but surely not under these circumstances,' she persisted doubtfully.

'Even more so now,' he assured her. 'She's in no pain and the ward is in an uproar when we all arrive. The rest of the patients call it the happy hour.'

'Well, if you're sure...'

'Of course I'm sure. Never been surer,' he said. 'You'll see what I mean when we get inside.'

And she did.

Victoria Davidson was propped against the pillows when they went into the ward. A big, grey-haired man was holding her hand at one side of the bed, and at the other side a youth who looked like a younger version of Rafe was smiling down on her.

She hadn't lost her hair, or if she had it had grown again, and it was of the same deep russet as Rafe's. She was painfully thin, transparent, almost, but the bright gaze that she bestowed upon them as they walked towards the bed had none of the fear of approaching death in it.

'Rafe!' she exclaimed softly, and there was all the love in the world in her voice.

As he bent to kiss her she cupped his face tenderly in skeletal hands, and Lucinda wished herself miles away. She couldn't intrude into this family's precious moments with someone they were shortly going to lose. But hardly had the thought been born than the sick woman was asking with a smile, 'And who is this that you've brought to see me?'

He turned and drew her nearer to the bed. 'Lucinda Beckman, Mum. Dr Lucinda Beckman from the Infirmary.'

And to herself, Rafe added, 'My mother, Victoria Davidson.' Indicating the grey-haired man, who hadn't yet spoken, he said, 'And my father, Albert. The young fellow at the other side of the bed is Miles, and my sister Zoe will be along shortly.

After Lucinda had shaken hands with everyone, Victoria Davidson said with the same easy good humour as her son, 'How nice of you to come to my party, Lucinda. It's due to start any moment. Zoe has gone to fetch the cake and wine, and two friends of Miles' are bringing their guitars. But first the children from the school where I taught before my illness are coming to sing for us.'

At that moment the door opened and a group of school-children entered in the company of a teacher, and those of the other patients who were well enough to take notice sat up in their beds expectantly.

As the children sang, their sweet young voices pealing forth, Lucinda thought, I don't believe I'm taking part in this. A party for a dying woman, surrounded by her loving family, and amongst them a man who is fast becoming far too important in my life.

There was tranquillity here. Grief was on hold. The matron smiling from the doorway knew it and so did everyone else. A dull ache in her chest told Lucinda that she was feeling envy. They all seemed so close, these Davidsons, golden-haired Zoe included.

Her only family was the trouble-prone Jake, and, fond as she was of him, he was no comfort to her when *she* needed someone.

The boys with the guitars had been instructed to keep it low, so as not to distress any patient not up to it, and when they'd played their repertoire Rafe said softly in her ear, 'If you're wondering about the music, Mum used to be a singer. Dad and I think that she got the cancer from passive smoking, as she spent a lot of time in theatres and clubs before cigarettes were banned in most public places.'

Lucinda nodded. It was possible. And yet deaths from cancer occurred where the victim had never smoked and had rarely been involved to any great extent in smoky atmospheres. The disease crept up on its sufferers like a silent scourge, and no one was safe from its tentacles.

As the party progressed, Victoria held her husband's hand tightly. Her bright brown eyes were fixed on the family that she soon must leave, and Lucinda marvelled at her composure.

'How can your mother be so serene?' she exclaimed wonderingly as they drove home in the borrowed Rover.

His smile was tender. 'She has a lot of inner strength, but I think the main reason is because she knows that we'll be all right. Dad will hold us together and each of us will look out for the other.'

'You're very lucky, Rafe,' she told him. 'My parents

died a long time ago, leaving just my brother and I. Jake
and I are close, but the unity of your family is something
else. I envy you.'

'You can see why I had to come back home, can't you?'
he said. 'Until a few days ago we were all together as a
family. It was only in the last week that Mum was admitted
to the hospice. It was at her own request. There is a possib-
ilty that she might come home again for a brief period,
but, as you could see, she's very weak.'

'Why did you take me there tonight?' she asked, curious
as to the reason, and praying that he wouldn't make light
of the question.

'My mother wanted to meet you.'

She goggled at him. 'But why? I wouldn't have thought
she knew I existed.'

'Of course she does. You've operated on a couple of the
children from her school.' He chuckled. 'And everybody's
heard of the bossy bone straightener.'

Disappointment was making her feel sick. Yet anyone
with a grain of commonsense would know there couldn't
be any other reason for Rafe's mother wanting to meet her.

A change of subject was called for. 'Where did the
cancer strike?' she asked.

'Originally in the lungs, and treatment halted it for a
couple of years. Then it was back, more vicious than
before.'

'So it has spread?'

'Mmm. I knew about it in the first instance, of course,
but it was the recurrence that my mother wanted to keep
from me, as she knew that the moment I realised that time
was running out I would be home.'

'And she was right.'

'Yes, she was. Though I feel that I am of little use.' He

sighed. 'Why didn't I specialise in cancer instead of cardiac surgery?'

'It wouldn't have made any difference,' she pointed out reasonably. 'There are so many times when nature has the last word, and all the medical skills in the world won't save the one who has been chosen to go.'

'Yes, I know that,' he agreed. 'It's just that it's so frustrating that I can help to save other people's lives and yet I'm useless when it comes to my own mother.'

When he brought the car to a halt outside her flat Rafe would have got out to see her inside, but Lucinda shook her head.

'Don't delay. Go home and get some rest. I've glanced at your schedule for tomorrow and there'll be no rest for you then. From what I've seen of your family, and your mother in particular, they won't want you falling apart.'

He eyed her for a moment, as if he would linger longer, but the sense of what she'd said was obvious. With a wry smile he raised his hand in farewell and departed, leaving her to return to her 'space capsule' with her head whirling with the day's events.

It was a foregone conclusion that she wouldn't sleep. There was too much to think about, too much to absorb. She'd been given a glimpse of what a real family was like tonight, and the thick skin that she'd grown to cover any weaknesses had cracked from the moment that Victoria Davidson had held her son.

That was something she wasn't going to forget, but something even more mind-blowing had happened in her office earlier in the day. She'd succumbed to what she'd expected to be a snatched kiss from an unlikely quarter and been amazed at her response.

Had it been so long since she'd been touched by an

attractive man that she'd behaved like a silly adolescent? She didn't know. But one thing she *did* know was that, whether he was right for her or not, she was falling in love with an idealistic, uncomplicated man, who belonged to a close-knit family.

Could *she* cope with that? The childless, loverless, career woman who was about as popular with most folk as a wet week in summer?

She shot upright in the bed. Of course she could! She'd always fought for what she wanted and this would be in a class of its own. Happiness was beckoning and she wasn't going to ignore it.

The next morning Lucinda lay back against the pillows and let her mind go back to the events of the previous day. There was an unfamiliar feeling inside her, barely recognisable because it was so long since she'd experienced it. It was anticipation.

For once the day ahead wasn't just looming as an exercise in working skills, and she couldn't remember when last she'd felt like that.

There'd been a time when every day was a challenge, an exciting prospect, but lack of success in personal relationships, the grinding, ever-present workload and the echoes of a needless tragedy that she'd had a part in had turned her into a workaholic.

It had taken a day like yesterday to remind her that she was missing out physically and emotionally, and she had Rafe to thank for catapulting her back into living.

But was *he* aware of it? Or had their explosive embrace in her office been all in a day's work to him? Had the introduction to his delightful family stemmed from pity, because he'd seen through the veneer of her cool confidence. . .guessed that she was lonely and frustrated underneath?

Stretching languorously on the cool satin sheets, she thrust the depressing thoughts aside and padded across to the wardrobe, where she eyed the clothes hanging there with a speculative eye.

What should she wear on the first day of her life as a new woman? Something startling and glamorous? Hardly, she told herself with a laughing grimace in the mirror. There would be eyebrows raised if she went slinking round the wards like an antiseptic cockatoo. But, as always, the inevitable white coat would conceal her plumage.

Bright, strong colours had always attracted her. Red, gold, emerald and brilliant turquoises complemented her dark colouring that came from Romany ancestors of long ago. The vivid colours were part of her defence. They helped to emphasise that the head of orthopaedics at the Infirmary was a confident, flamboyant woman and, having put up the screen, she'd been content to hide behind it.

Having limited herself to a scarlet blazer, crisp white blouse and black skirt, she went into her chromium-plated kitchen and made herself a quick breakfast. As she munched on a piece of toast, Lucinda looked around her.

Recalling Rafe's amazed amusement of the night before, she supposed that it did look like an extension of an operating theatre, with its cold, clinical, decor, but it suited her purpose and she'd never thought to question it until she'd seen his expression on entering her abode.

She could imagine the Davidsons having one of those big farmhouse-type kitchens, dominated by a huge cooking range and with a large pine table in the centre. There would be cast-iron pans hanging symmetrically above one's head, and a larder full of home-made chutney, jams and bottled fruit.

Stop fantasising, woman! she scolded herself. You should be more concerned about what kind of a night that poor woman has had than what kind of a kitchen she's got.

And on that sombre note she picked up her briefcase and sallied forth.

Ethan Lassiter, the manager of Springfield Hospital, came on the phone the moment she set foot in her office to say that one of her post-operative patients who had been transferred into his care was giving cause for concern, and would she call and see him?

'Of course,' she said immediately. 'Who is it?'

'Simon Jackson. You gave him a new knee last week.'

Her heart sank. She didn't need to be reminded who he was. He was one of the most difficult patients she'd had in a long time, and if there was one person she didn't want having any post-operative hiccups it was he.

An aggressive, authoritative forty-year-old, unmarried and likely to remain so if his personality was anything to go by, he had been awkward from the word go.

On the occasion of his first visit as an outpatient at the Infirmary he had been seen by her second-in-command, John Adams, a skilful young doctor and happy family man. When Simon Jackson had discovered that there was someone else above him, namely herself, he'd insisted arrogantly that he wanted to be seen by the organ-grinder. . . not the monkey.

Furious at the insult to John she had slammed into the cubicle where the disruptive bachelor had been waiting and said in chilling tones, 'I believe that you insisted on seeing me?'

'What?' he'd exclaimed. '*You're* the top dog here?'

'That is so,' she'd informed him with continuing frost. 'It looks as if your fanatical sporting activities in the past have brought about severe arthritis of the knee, so *I* shall be doing the joint replacement. . .as you have requested.'

He'd been silent for a moment, and then had said ungraciously, 'I'd rather have a male doctor.'

'Really?' she'd commented with feigned surprise. 'But you've just had the attentions of one of your own sex and refused them. So you're going to have to put up with me.'

And now, according to what the nursing manager at Springfield was saying, it looked as if stroppy Simon was to be part of the one per cent of post-operative patients who developed an infection at the site of the new joint.

When Lucinda appeared at the side of Simon Jackson's bed, with Ethan and Isobel Graham, the senior sister, in attendance, she was met with a spate of abuse, and resentment rose in her.

She'd been looking forward to the day, and it had barely had the chance to get under way before she was getting the sharp end of the tongue from the original male chauvinist.

Ethan Lassiter's face had darkened, and before Lucinda could retaliate, he said with smooth authority, 'Since I asked Dr Beckman to come here to see you I've discovered that there is a possibility that you haven't been taking the medication we've given you.'

'Of course I have,' the complainant blustered.

'You've been seen flushing tablets down the toilet on two occasions.'

'If that is the case, the onset of a chronic septic infection is not surprising,' Lucinda told Simon Jackson. 'On examination of the inflamed state of your knee, that is what it appears to be. We always prescribe antibiotic drugs for ten days after prosthetic surgery, and if you haven't been taking them, this is the result.'

'Oh. I see. So you're trying to put the blame for a bungled job onto me!' he shouted.

'Not at all. You've been your own worst enemy by ignoring the medication you've been given,' she admonished. 'You'd better not continue with that sort of stupidity or I'm going to have to open the knee up again and remove any dead bone, cement, and the metal parts that go to make up the prosthesis.'

The colour had left his face at the prospect, but he still wasn't prepared to admit to any blame. 'I didn't take the tablets because after the first day they made me feel nauseous.'

'And how do you think having your knee opened up again is going to make you feel?' Ethan Lassiter asked grimly, and for once the difficult patient had nothing to say.

As they walked back to the hospital manager's office, Lucinda said, 'He *has* to take the antibiotics, Ethan. Even if you have to sit on him and hold his nose while they go down. There are signs of chronic infection, but hopefully immediate dosing will halt it.'

'The percentage of post-operative patients who get that sort of thing is so small, due to the precautions we take, that I could hardly believe it when you told me the symptoms. But men like Simon Jackson are a law unto themselves, I'm afraid.'

Inside she was begging, Let me get to an uncomplicated man. . .a man like Rafe. . .who doesn't create problems just for the fun of it. I've had enough of surly, difficult types.

As she put the Mercedes out onto the road that led to the Infirmary, for once in her life she was glad to see

the back of the small cottage-type hospital, with its solid
redbrick structure, neat gardens, and the stream running
through them that had given the place its name.

CHAPTER FOUR

THE first person Lucinda saw when she got back to the Infirmary was Bevan Marsland, deep in conversation with one of the paediatric registrars in the hospital foyer.

She groaned. The day was going from bad to worse. What was *he* doing on the premises? Bevan was based at Springfield, along with running the village practice. It was rare for him to grace the corridors of the Infirmary.

He looked across as she made her way to the lift and gave a curt nod. In return Lucinda observed him with guarded dark eyes. Cassandra had said that she was working on her husband to make him drop his antagonism towards herself, but if his present affability was anything to go by, it was a slow process.

But she'd better things to think about than Bevan Marsland, in the shape of a cardiac surgeon with hair like dark gold and a smile that made the earth move in spite of there being a lot of sorrow inside him.

Her assistant, John Adams, so scathingly passed over by the belligerent Simon Jackson, was taking the clinic in her absence. After checking that there were no problems needing her attention, Lucinda made her way to the cardiac unit.

If she needed an excuse for seeking Rafe out she had one. . . Anne Tavistock, the sister from orthopaedics with the failing heart. But she was hoping that there would be no call for excuses, that he would be as anxious to see her as she was him.

Sir Thomas was doing his rounds when she got there, striding pompously from bed to bed with a senior sister and a general nurse following behind like bridesmaids. There was no sign of the man she'd come to see, and when she enquired of another member of staff she was told that Dr Davidson was in Theatre.

She sighed. What a frustrating morning it was turning out to be. There was nothing left to do but go back to her own patch and get on with the day's duties.

'Will you ask him to ring me when he's free?' she asked of the young nurse who'd volunteered the information.

Yes, Dr Beckman,' the girl said obediently.

Because her visit to Springfield had taken a slice out of the morning, lunchtime was upon her before she knew it, and there had been no phone call from Rafe.

Feeling edgy, Lucinda went outside into the dank winter morning to check that the bike was still there, and sure enough it was, so at least he hadn't left the premises.

You're behaving like a neurotic nymphomaniac, she told herself wryly as she went back inside. With your track record you should have more sense. You know that men run a mile when they discover how confident and clever you are. Your type isn't in fashion. Men are looking for clever women, all right, but they mustn't be cleverer than them. Just because Rafe Davidson has shown some liking for your company, it doesn't mean that he's gone to order top hat and tails!

He came into the staff restaurant just as she was finishing her lunch, and her eyes fixed on him as if he was going to disappear and she must memorise him for ever.

Watching him, she saw that for once he seemed to lack his usual easy manner and her heartbeat quickened.

Maybe there was bad news about his mother.

'Hi,' he said as he stopped by her table and deposited his tray. 'How are you this morning?'

'Fine,' she told him, knowing it to be true now that he had appeared. 'And how about you?'

He grimaced. 'It's been a hellish morning in Theatre. The only good thing is that I haven't had Sir Tom pontificating in my ear.' The grimace became a grin. 'And calling me "my boy"!'

'What was wrong in Theatre?' she asked.

He rolled his eyes heavenwards. 'I was just sewing up the chest wall after replacing a stenotic valve when a patient was brought in with a stab wound to the heart. Some sort of domestic affray, and the carving knife had been used.'

Lucinda sighed. 'When will the public realise that we have enough to do correcting the vagaries of nature, without self-inflicted problems?'

He nodded. 'The guy only just got to us in time. The wound was deep; even though the gash has been repaired there's still the risk of infection. And guess what? When I came out of Theatre the police were waiting for a statement regarding his condition.'

'When I saw you looking so solemn in the food queue I thought you'd had bad news about your mother,' she told him.

He shook his head. 'No. I called in at the hospice on my way here this morning and she'd had a reasonable night.' As she smiled her relief he went on to say, 'When I came out of Theatre there was a note waiting for me from Bevan.

"Apparently he'd called in to see me, and when I wasn't available he scribbled a note to say that he and Cassanndra are holding a party in my honour on Saturday night. A sort

of 'getting to know you' affair, which I think is very decent
of them. It isn't due to start until nine o'clock, so I'll be
able to join my family for the happy hour first."

'Yes, it is decent of them,' she said flatly, remembering
Bevan's bleak acknowledgement when they'd seen each
other earlier, and knowing that there was no likelihood of
her name being on the guest list.

'They've suggested that I bring a companion of my
own choice,' he was saying when she tuned back into the
conversation, 'and I thought of you.'

'Me!' she gasped as the colour rose in her face. 'Oh, I
don't know. I'm not acquainted with the Marslands all
that well.'

He was eyeing her in surprise. 'But you were at the
christening!'

'Yes, I know, but I was only an afterthought.'

'Well, so what? You can still come. They're not stipulat-
ing who I can or cannot bring.'

Not at the moment, she thought grimly. But just wait
until Bevan finds out!

'Come on, Lucinda,' he wheedled. 'Come out of your
chromium-plated tower for once.'

There was nothing she would have liked more than to
be his guest at a party. . .but not this one! And yet why not?
Cassandra had insisted that her husband was mellowing
towards her, in spite of his continuing dour attitude. It
would be an opportunity to see if it was true. Even if there
was no improvement it wouldn't affect Rafe's night.

If she had to weigh the pleasure of spending the evening
in Rafe's company against a few black looks from Bevan
it would be the first choice every time, and so, turning the
full brilliance of her gratification on him, she said lightly,
'Yes, all right. Why not? And now I've got something to

ask of you,' she went on with a lilt in her voice at the thought of the forthcoming event. 'And I'm afraid that it has nothing to do with parties or pleasure.'

'What is it?' he asked slowly.

'You recall that I went to see a member of my staff yesterday? Anne Tavistock, who is suffering from severe heart failure?'

'Ah, yes, I remember the patient. Sir Tom has her down for a transplant.'

'Yes, so he said. But I keep remembering what you said about this new heart shrink surgery and I wonder if it would be suitable for Anne. I've done some reading up on it since you mentioned it, and the fact that there is no life-long dependence on drugs after the operation is marvellous. As is the much shorter recovery time.'

He pursed his lips thoughtfully. 'Yes. It's an incredible breakthrough in heart surgery. So far the trials of it have been limited to the Bristol area, which, as we are both aware, isn't far from here. Two other hospitals in the UK have been chosen to try it out during the coming year, but, as I pointed out when we discussed it earlier, the Infirmary isn't one of them.

'Anne would have to be accepted by one of these other hospitals for her to have access to the treatment, and, as is always the case, that's where money comes into it. Would another area pay for the operation?'

'A transfer of funds, maybe?' she suggested.

'Possibly,' he agreed. 'Leave it with me, Lucinda. I'll see what I can find out without treading on Sir Tom's toes too much.'

She reached out and squeezed his hand. 'I knew you would say that. You're a nice man, Rafe.'

He didn't return the pressure, but just looked down on

their joined hands and said, 'That makes me sound rather boring and predictable, and I'd like to bet that is how you see me, eh, Lucinda?'

She smiled. 'You'd be surprised how I see you. At the first opportunity I'll enlighten you.' She got to her feet reluctantly. 'I must go, Rafe. My lunch-hour was over before you appeared. I can't chide my staff for not being back on time if I'm guilty of the same offence, can I?'

He gave her his quirky smile and it was like the sun breaking through cloud after Simon Jackson and Bevan. 'No, you can't. Go and get back to your broken bones and I'll be in touch to arrange about Saturday.'

She didn't want to leave him. It would have been nice to linger, to talk about themselves instead of every other subject under the sun, but she consoled herself that there was Saturday to look forward to.

That was the bonus that this day had brought, and, resisting the impulse to bend down and kiss the lips that had held her spellbound only twenty-four hours before, she left the restaurant with her confident swaying stride. Her ebony hair lay smooth against her head in a neat twist and the red blazer, straight black skirt and sheer stockings became the glowing flag of her sensuality.

On the night of the party Rafe rang at a quarter to nine to say that he'd been delayed at the hospital and had only just arrived for his nightly visit to his mother.

'Would you mind very much going without me?' he asked. 'I know it's asking a bit much, when you're supposed to be my guest, but as it is all in my honour I do feel that one of us should put in an appearance at the beginning.'

'No! I'll wait for you,' she said immediately. There was

no way she wanted to walk into the Marsland house without him. She knew that she would receive a warm welcome from Cassandra, but it was Bevan and the rest of them that she didn't want to face.

The taciturn GP couldn't very well object if she arrived on the arm of the guest of honour, but if he were to see her strolling in uninvited and, for his part, unwelcome, it would be a different matter.

Added to that, there would be sniggers amongst the rest of the hospital crowd who had been invited at the sight of La Beckman, on her own as usual.

'Please, Lucinda,' he coaxed. 'It isn't as if you won't know anyone there. I'm the one who's the stranger to most of them, and I've got my mum here getting all upset because I'm letting you down. If you won't go on ahead she will insist that I leave this very minute to pick you up.'

'You drive a hard bargain,' she said soberly. He would never know how hard. 'But, as the last thing in the world I would want to do is distress your mother, I'll do as you ask.'

'You're a sweetie,' he said softly in her ear. 'And I promise I'll make it up to you before the night is out.'

'You will?'

'You can bet on it,' he teased, and at that moment the excitement at the thought of a new relationship outweighed everything else.

In contrast to the vivid colours that she was so fond of Lucinda had decided to wear white for the party that the Marslands were giving for Rafe—a long-sleeved dress of white wool crêpe that clung to her lissom curves and made her skin glow.

She had relieved it with antique gold jewellery and the

final effect was stunning. So much so that dreading her solitary arrival at the party, she began to wish that she'd dressed down instead of up. But there was only a matter of minutes left before she must set off, and as Rafe had been so concerned that she be there at the start changing her clothes was out of the question.

And why should she? she reasoned, as the car moved smoothly along the road that led to the village where Cassandra and Bevan lived. 'When nervous, dress up' had always been her motto, but for a few seconds back there in her bedroom she'd had a sudden urge to make herself inconspicuous, so that she could creep in unobserved.

She was hardly going to be able to do that, though, was she? Not when she was going to have to inform her host and hostess that she was there not by their invitation but by Rafe's.

'Lucinda!' Cassandra cried when she opened the door to her. 'What a lovely surprise!'

There was no dubious astonishment or embarrassing silence here. Lucinda knew that the other woman was genuinely pleased to see her and she hoped that nothing would change when she'd explained her presence.

'I'm here because of Rafe,' she said in her usual direct manner. 'He said that you'd told him to bring a guest and for some reason he invited me. But unfortunately he's been delayed and suggested that I came on ahead.'

Cassandra's pleasure certainly hadn't abated at the reason for her presence, but now it was combined with astonishment. 'Really! Well, do make yourself at home. Can I get you a drink?'

'Yes, please. A white wine and soda if you have it,' she said breathlessly, with the feeling that she'd gabbled out the reason for her presence in a most undignified manner.

As she stood, glass in hand, regaining her poise, oblivious to the fact that she was the most striking-looking woman in the room, Lucinda was praying that Rafe wouldn't be long. She could cope as long as Bevan kept away from her, but it was a vain hope.

She turned her head and he was there beside her. 'Cassie tells me that you are Rafe's partner for the night,' he said with cold politeness. 'I wasn't aware that you were acquainted.'

Anger sparked inside her. He'd said it as if she had leprosy, or something similarly to be avoided, but there was too much at stake to lose her cool. For one thing she was a guest in his house, and for another he was a friend of Rafe's, but under other circumstances she wouldn't have kept quiet.

It was grossly unfair of him to put her at a disadvantage whenever she saw him. Darren was dead; nothing could alter that. But she'd suffered too. The regret she'd carried around with her all this time had taken the edge off everything she did, everything she'd achieved, but Bevan didn't want to know about that. Only Cassandra understood, and she had just as much cause to condemn her as he had.

'We come into contact occasionally at the Infirmary,' she told him, with the cool self-possession that was her armour in times of stress. 'And if you remember I met him at your daughter's christening.'

'Rafe is a very special guy,' he said grimly. 'On the surface he might seem lightweight, but underneath he's warm and caring and one of the best doctors I've ever worked with. I've watched him operate under horrendous conditions out in Bosnia without batting an eyelid, and I wouldn't want him to. . .'

He paused meaningfully and all her good intentions went

by the board. 'You wouldn't want him contaminated by someone like me. . .is *that* what you were going to say?'

'You seem to have got the idea.'

'And is that surprising?' she snapped. 'After years of your antagonism!' She was past caring now. Nothing mattered except the pain around her heart and the dismay that anyone could find her so repellent.

'I'm sorry I came here tonight.' She picked up her bag and gloves. 'Please give your friend my apologies when he arrives.'

When she got back to the flat Lucinda flung the white dress and the underwear that she'd worn beneath it into a corner and threw herself onto the bed, where she lay stiff with misery.

What a fiasco, she thought grimly. She should have obeyed her instincts and not allowed Rafe to persuade her to go alone. Bevan Marsland would have backed off if they'd been together, but that wasn't to guarantee that he wouldn't be saying his piece the first moment he had Rafe alone. And by walking out of the party she'd offered him the opportunity on a plate.

By now Rafe would have been well and truly warned off her, and she had no defence. Bevan was an honourable man. He would only tell Rafe the truth. But in this instance the truth wasn't a pleasant thing.

Her doorbell rang at half past one in the morning, and she knew that there was only one person who would be calling on her at this hour.

It had taken the intrusive buzz to bring her out of her stupor and now, with a snowy bedsheet draped around her, and her face whiter than the sheet, she went to face him.

'And so what was it all about, Lucinda?' he said quietly

as he strode past her. 'I would have been here before, but as I was the guest of honour I couldn't very well leave before the end of the party. . .unlike yourself. I was only minutes behind you, and if Bevan hadn't assured me that you *had* put in an appearance I might have doubted your being there at all.'

'If you've been discussing me with your over-protective friend I'm surprised that you need to ask *me* for an explanation.' she said sourly.

'I'm not with you. . .?'

Lucinda stared at him. 'You mean to say that he hasn't told you that I am to be avoided?'

He shook his head blankly. 'No.'

'You surprise me. Then perhaps I'd better do it for him, as he will be telling you sooner or later. His young brother was killed some years ago in a drunken prank that I was the instigator of,' she said tonelessly, 'and he's never forgiven me.

'Darren, Cassandra and I were all medical students together. He and Cassandra had been dating, but *I* wanted him, too, and he ditched her for me. We'd been to a party and had too much to drink and I dared him to climb a church steeple.'

Her eyes darkened as the horror of it came back. 'He got almost to the top and lost his footing.' The sight of Darren falling through space and the dull thud as he hit the ground was something she would remember to her dying day.

'I see,' Rafe said slowly. 'It was a tragedy that came from drink and high spirits in your wild youth.' There was a half-smile on his face and her heart began to lighten. '*That* is how you got your reputation for being a wild woman, I presume?'

'Yes. And the result of all that was that I tried to reform by marrying a man old enough to be my father.'

There was tension in his jawline now. 'And what happened to him?'

'A heart attack.'

The expression on his face told her that she wasn't out of the woods yet. She almost expected him to comment that he wasn't surprised, but he was harking back to Bevan.

'And so why is my friend Bevan so unforgiving about what was more of a stupid prank than real wickedness?'

Lucinda took a deep breath. 'Because he mistakenly blamed Cassandra for Darren's death and I didn't put him straight. He and his parents were living in Australia at the time, and when they came over he mistook her for the girl who'd dared his brother to climb the steeple. I heard him accuse her, but kept quiet because I was so ashamed.'

Rafe opened his mouth to speak but she forestalled him. 'I haven't finished yet.' Better to go on to the bitter end than leave anything unsaid she decided wretchedly. 'Darren had made Cassie pregnant and she was left to bring Mark up on her own. She'd been afraid to tell the Marslands they had a grandson, and Bevan he had a nephew, because of the way he'd ranted at her.'

'And then a couple of years ago Bevan came back to this area to fill in for a friend of his as GP in the village. He didn't recognise her as the girl he'd torn a strip off at his brother's funeral and he and Cassandra fell in love. But guess who told him who she was, and how she'd borne his brother's child?'

'You!' he said stonily.

'Yes, me. I was too miserable to think straight after losing my husband, and I blurted it out one night when we were all together. He couldn't forgive her for not telling

him that his brother was Mark's father, and as he still
believed that she was involved in the accident, they nearly
split up.'

'So you really do have something to answer for,' he
breathed.

'Yes, I do,' she told him steadily. 'Though fortunately
it all came right in the end for them.'

'But no thanks to you.'

'No. No thanks to me, and that is why I've never been
one of Bevan Marsland's favourite people. Cassandra for-
gave me long ago, but not he.'

There was still a glimmer of hope inside her as she said
stiffly, 'And now that I've told you all about my murky
past can we get on with *our* lives, Rafe?'

'Sure,' he agreed, and her heart leapt, but it plummeted
just as quickly as he said, 'I'll get on with mine...and
you can get on with yours. But don't expect them to be
intertwined, Lucinda. You did a despicable thing to
Cassandra Marsland.'

'I was attracted to you by your confidence, your dedication, and most of all by what I thought was your integrity.
I've had an unfortunate experience with a member of your
sex and am normally wary, but for once I made a snap
judgement. I won't do it again.'

Before she could protest or explain he turned on his heel
and went.

Throughout what was left of the night her feelings were
a mixture of anger and despair. Part of the anger was at
her stupidity for allowing one passionate embrace and a
visit to a sickroom make her lower her defences, and the
rest of it was directed at Rafe for his reaction to her reluctant confession.

She'd been mistaken to think that his easy ways indi-

cated an uncomplicated man, she thought wretchedly, as
another grey November day was born. He was an
idealist. . .a man of principle. . .and he'd gone away thinking her to be the lowest of the low.

He wasn't to know that she'd lost her parents and been
left with a difficult young brother to cope with. Then, when
she'd thought an anchor had appeared in the form of the
caring Piers, he too had been taken.

All right, no one knew better than she the wrong she'd
done Cassandra Marsland, but they were friends now, and
that was about the only comforting thing in the whole
sorry mess.

By the time she got to Infirmary on Monday morning she
had made one decision. Nothing mind-bending, but it
would be a means of clarifying her thoughts and licking
her wounds. A call to a local travel agent before she started
her clinic resulted in a booking for a two-week solitary
vacation in Venice, commencing the next day.

Lucinda had never gone away at short notice before.
She was too committed to the job. But in this instance
John and the rest of her team could cope perfectly well
without her. If anything really tricky came up it would
have to wait until she came back.

Rafe's bike wasn't in its usual place and she was glad
of it. If she could manage to avoid him today, tomorrow
would come soon enough. And she was praying that by
the time she came back from holiday she would have sorted
her life out in one way or another.

She had a Burmese student doctor sitting in with her for
today's clinic, and as a nurse ushered in the first patient
the trainee eyed the woman carefully.

A mother of two small children, who were clinging to

her fretfully, she had fallen heavily onto her outstretched hand and sustained a fracture of the scaphoid—the outermost bone on the thumb side of the hand.

It was a common enough fracture, and diagnosable by the amount of tenderness between the two most prominent tendons at the base of the thumb on the back of the hand. The injury was going to require a plaster cast, and, after reassuring the shaken woman that although inconvenient the injury wasn't serious, Lucinda passed her on to a small room at the end of the corridor to have the necessary plaster applied.

It was a rarer problem that followed her. A small girl had been sent by her GP to have her shoulder examined. The scapula, or shoulderblade, hadn't descended on one side, and it was giving the child's neck a webbed appearance.

After inviting the student to examine the little patient for himself Lucinda asked him how *he* would correct it and was impressed when he came up with the right answer.

He suggested that the defective shoulder blade should be osteotomised. In other words, its shape to be altered instead of releasing the inner muscles, a procedure sometimes used.

When she asked him for a reason why, it was clear that he'd done his homework. An osteotomy would allow more movement down the affected side of the body and improve the cosmetic appearance, he told her.

'Well done,' she said crisply, and he got to his feet and gave her a stiff little bow.

Her hopes of avoiding Rafe were dashed when they almost collided as he was coming out of Theatre, and as they stopped and faced each other she saw that the warmth was still missing from the dark hazel eyes looking into hers.

'Hello, Lucinda,' he said with frosty politeness. 'I heard your secretary telling someone earlier that you're off to Venice on vacation tomorrow. It's a bit sudden, isn't it?'

'Maybe,' she said, with an equal lack of warmth, 'but, if I remember rightly, last night you were at pains to point out that from now on we go our separate ways. In that event what I choose to do, and where I choose to go, have nothing to do with you.'

'I see. In other words you don't want to admit that you're running away?'

'I. . .am. . .not. . .running. . .away,' she said grittily. 'And if I am, who is better experienced in taking the coward's way out than myself?' With a toss of her dark hair she pushed past him and went on her way.

CHAPTER FIVE

ON THE flight to Venice Lucinda read, slept, picked at the food on offer, and generally did everything except think about Rafe.

Before leaving she'd arranged for flowers to be sent to his mother. Victoria Davidson had asked her to go to see her again and she'd promised she would, fully expecting the visit to be in the company of her son.

But it wasn't going to be like that, and so the flowers were to make up for her non-appearance. If anything should happen to the sick woman while she was away, it would be just one more thing to feel guilty about.

She'd also made time to phone Jake, to let him know that she was going to be out of the country and to check that all was well with he and Melanie.

'We're fine, Luce,' he'd said reassuringly, and had then turned her sigh of relief into a groan as he'd gone on to say, 'Except that we're a bit strapped for cash.'

'And what's new about that?' she'd asked drily, before relenting to say that she would put a cheque in the post.

There had been one more loose end to be tied before she left, and she had been loath to do it as it involved speaking to Rafe. It would have been easier if she'd mentioned it when they'd bumped into each other earlier, but sadly they'd been engaged in verbal sparring again and it had gone out of her mind.

'I thought you'd already left the country,' he'd said when she'd rung him at his parents' home this morning.

'Did you? Sorry to disappoint you. I'm due to leave for the airport shortly, but first I thought I'd ask if you've anything to report on Anne Tavistock's problem. I'm very concerned about her.'

There had been silence for a moment, and when he'd broken it his manner hadn't been as aloof. . .but neither had it been gushing.

'I appreciate that you're concerned,' he'd allowed, 'and I've spoken to Sir Tom about her. He's not too pleased that you're interfering in our department, but he's agreed to see her again. If we both think she'll benefit from the heart shrink surgery then we'll try to do a deal with one of the hospitals where she can have it done. Does that satisfy you?'

'Yes, just as long as you don't let the grass grow under your feet,' she'd told him coolly. 'Anne hasn't got that sort of time, and if Sir Thomas Simmons isn't pleased with me he can join the club.'

'Meaning?'

'Along with Bevan Marsland and yourself.'

'I see. And how *did* you expect me to react to the sordid little story you were forced to tell me?'

She'd been glad that he hadn't been able to see her ravaged face as she'd flipped back, 'With tolerance, maybe. . .fulfilling your role as Mr Nice Guy?'

'So we're disappointed in each other?'

'You could say that,' she told him bleakly. 'And now I must go. My taxi will be here shortly.'

'Fair enough. . .and Lucinda?'

'Ye-e-es?' she'd asked warily.

'Have a coffee for me on St Mark's Square.'

'I hate you, Rafe Davidson,' she'd said. 'And I might just see what's on offer in the Italian job centres.'

'What, and deprive the folk in the Midlands of Beckman the Bone Woman? You can't take your pique out on the suffering majority.'

She'd put the phone down on that note, resisting the urge to tell him that nobody cared a damn about *her* suffering, and that the parry and thrust conversation they'd just been involved in hadn't alleviated it any.

Her stay in Venice lasted just three days. On the first day Lucinda was the tourist, hiding behind dark glasses with guidebook in hand. She had coffee on St Mark's Square, as Rafe had suggested, with an orchestra playing beside her and the Doge's Palace nearby.

She crossed the famous Bridge of Sighs and saw the dungeons where the unfortunates had rotted away in bygone days before being executed.

She shopped on the Rialto Bridge spanning the Grand Canal, and watched the glass-blowers working at their furnaces down one of the many narrow walkways.

And she had a solitary ride in a gondola, and turned her head away as a similar craft passed by, bedecked with flowers and satin cushions, on which sat a bride and her new husband.

On the second day she gave up the pretence and moped around the streets and myriad waterways, telling herself angrily that she'd been out of her mind to come to a place like this in her present state.

Romance was everywhere she looked. The reflection of the pastel-shaded palaces edging the Grand Canal shimmered up from its waters. Beautiful olive-skinned brides seemed to be spilling out of every ancient church. Glittering showcases of exquisite glass were everywhere she looked, and the shops were full of fine jewels and couturier clothes.

Venice was a place for a honeymoon, she thought sombrely. . .not an exile. She was the perfect example of a fish out of water, although she needn't have been. There were plenty of admiring glances cast her way but she chose to ignore them.

For years she'd thought that the man for her hadn't been created, and then it had all changed. She'd met a man called Rafe and from being dubious about him she'd swung the other way and been captivated by his easy ways, his humour and his looks. But what good had it done her?

Bevan Marsland might not know it, but he'd finally got even. He'd made her tell Rafe about the shaming past and by doing so she had been left desolate again in the despairing present.

At the end of her third day she was enquiring about flights back, and on the morning of the fourth she returned to England with the feeling that she was making a prize fool of herself.

Rafe would think she couldn't keep away from him. . . which was true, and anyone else who happened to see her would find it incredible that she'd come back so soon from a well-earned vacation. The only thing to do was stay indoors. . .keep out of sight.

She went out in the evenings when the streets were dark and deserted, like some stalker of the night. It would have been amusing if it hadn't been so depressing, but there was no way she could appear at the Infirmary and take up the reins again before her leave was over. They would think she was crazy and she supposed she was, skulking in her flat like a criminal.

On the Wednesday of the second week, when freedom was almost in sight, she was going out for food in the late evening. As she stepped through her door into the corridor she was grabbed from the side and forced up against the wall.

Her scream of alarm and an amazed male voice exclaiming, 'Lucinda!' came simultaneously. As her cry trailed away Rafe hissed, 'Where the devil have *you* come from? I saw the lights on in your flat and came up to investigate as the porter was nowhere to be seen.'

She was still in his grasp and happy to be so, near enough to see stubble on his chin and the amber flecks in the irises of what, at that moment, were stormy brown eyes, and ridiculously she said, 'You have lovely teeth.'

He gave an exasperated sigh and growled, 'All the better to bite you with, Red Riding Hood, but I'm not here for a chat about my orthodontics. I want to know where you've come from?'

'Well, Venice, obviously. I got an earlier flight.'

'So you came back today.'

'Yes,' she fibbed without batting an eyelid.

'Why?'

'No reason. I'd seen all there was to see.'

He was eyeing her dubiously. 'What, in Venice? I doubt it, but if that's your story, I suppose you're sticking to it.'

'Why were you outside my flat?' she asked warily, wondering if she'd been spotted on one of her nocturnal excursions.

The colour rose in his face. 'I was passing on my way home and happened to glance up.'

'I see,' she said, trying to keep the disappointment out of her voice. 'So you weren't sitting on the doorstep pining for me? Wishing you hadn't sent me packing?

'No,' he said flatly. 'I rarely say things I don't mean.'

'Or *do* things you don't mean. . .like this,' she said. And, deciding that another misdemeanour wouldn't make all that much difference to his opinion of her, she placed her slender hand behind his neck and, pulling his face down to hers, kissed him meltingly on the lips.

His response told her that whether he was disenchanted with her or not she had lit a fuse, and as it sparked and then became fire they were moulding themselves to each other, their mouths hungry, her hands raking his hair, his grasp fierce with the longing to possess.

But in the middle of it he became still, gave a long, shuddering sigh and stepped back, his arms falling away as he did so.

'I must be insane letting you sidetrack me like this,' he said. 'We've nothing in common. . .'

'Except this,' she murmured, still mesmerised by his nearness. 'And our profession.'

His face became grave. 'Yes, our profession—which reminds me that I have something to tell you.'

Lucinda felt a shiver run down her spine at his tone and was grieved that the passion they'd just shared had been put to one side so quickly.

'What is it?' she asked abruptly.

'Anne Tavistock died yesterday.'

'Oh, no!' she wailed.

'I'm afraid so,' he said soberly. 'In spite of the medication she was on, the heart just gave up. I'd been in touch with the authorities at Bristol to see if they could help and was awaiting their reply, but. . .'

'So you *did* do as I asked.'

'Of course. You don't think I would ignore a suggestion of that sort, especially coming from *you*.'

'So I'm not entirely beyond the pale?'

'I don't ever remember saying that you were.'

'Oh, no, but it didn't take you long to side with your friend, Bevan.'

'I'm quite capable of making my own judgements, thank you,' he said quietly. 'Now I'd better get going. It's been a long day and it must have been the same for you, waiting around in the airports and suchlike.'

'Yes, it has,' she murmured, and, quickly changing the subject, she added, 'I'll walk down with you. I'm out of milk and bread and was going to the delicatessen when you grabbed me.'

The porter was back at his desk when they walked through the entrance hall and, to her chagrin, he remarked cheerfully, 'The dry cleaning that you gave me on Monday is back, Dr Beckman.'

'Er. . .thank you. I'll pick it up on my return,' she mumbled, avoiding the accusing gaze of her companion.

'So you came back today, did you?' he said once they were outside. 'You seem to be having trouble with the truth again.' When she didn't answer, he exploded, 'For God's sake, Lucinda! Why did you have to lie to me?'

'Why do you think?' she flared. 'Because I felt a fool coming back before the holiday was up.'

He was watching her with a strange intentness. 'So when *did* you come home?'

'About a week ago.'

'But why?'

'Why do you think?' she snapped. 'Because I was missing a man who thinks I'm some sort of low-life? And before your opinion of me gets any lower. . .how is your mother? We've been so busy haranguing each other I haven't had the chance to ask.'

The question seemed to bring them onto an even footing, and his aloofness disappeared as he shook his head sombrely. 'She loved the flowers you sent. . .said they reminded her of you. . .bright and beautiful.

'But she's bad. . .very bad. I spent last night with her and Dad and Zoe are staying with her tonight. I've a full day at the Infirmary tomorrow, but after that I'm taking leave as I want to be with her every moment I can.'

Lucinda nodded. 'Of course.'

She was tempted to say that she would go to visit Victoria, but it was no time for strangers to be butting in on their sorrow so she held her tongue.

She wanted to hold him, to offer comfort, but he needed a different thing from their wild embrace of a few moments ago. In his grief for his mother Rafe needed arms around him of someone he could trust and respect. . .not hers, and with that knowledge searing her heart she turned to face the night wind and said in a low voice, 'You'll be in my thoughts, which is perhaps not the best comfort in the world, but nevertheless you will be there.'

On that note she left him, walking quickly to where the lights of the late-night delicatessen glowed in the darkness.

The next morning Lucinda went to see Anne Tavistock's family. It was a sad occasion and did nothing to improve her mood of melancholy.

'A Dr Davidson came round earlier,' Anne's sorrowing husband said, 'and he told me how you'd asked him to try to get some new kind of treatment for Anne. It was good of you, Dr Beckman. It's just a pity that her heart didn't hold out that long.'

'It is, indeed,' she agreed. 'She will be sadly missed by all of us in the orthopaedic unit.'

'Aye, I know,' he said, 'but not as much as she'll be missed here.'

'No, of course,' she acknowledged tactfully.

After staying to find out the funeral arrangements, so that the hospital might be represented, she left, thinking that death was par for the course in health care, but it hurt just as much as it did for everyone else when one knew the person who had gone.

And that thought brought to mind Victoria Davidson once more, and Rafe, who must soon lose his mother. But she told herself there was no point in getting involved as she was well and truly on the sidelines as far as he was concerned.

She hadn't wanted it to be that way, but the past had caught up with her again. No matter how hard she worked...how hard she fought for recognition amongst those she mixed with, it was always lurking. The dreadful thing was that if anyone but Rafe had been involved, she would done what she always did, put on her bold face and ignored it.

But it would seem that the woman for him must be whiter than white, cleaner than clean, and she wondered wretchedly if *he'd* ever done anything that he was ashamed of.

Yet he wouldn't have, would he? His family were there for him. He'd been brought up in a house full of love and togetherness, and with his mother's going nothing would change.

He wouldn't be left to fend for himself with no one to turn to and with a young brother to bring up. Thinking of Jake, she decided that it was time she spoke to him again.

'Thanks for the cheque, Luce,' were his first words, and then he went on to say, 'We thought you weren't due back until the weekend?'

'Er...yes...well, I decided that I'd had enough,' she

said casually. 'The bright perfection of Italy is not quite so much in evidence in November, I'm afraid, but I enjoyed the rest. And now tell me, how are Melanie and the bump.'

'All right as far as we know. She's gone to antenatal this morning so we might know more when she comes back. I couldn't go with her as I had a lecture.'

Lucinda was smiling. He sounded older and more responsible, and she thought whimsically that maybe the thought of fatherhood was having an effect. . .and if it was, she was glad.

The phone rang in the early afternoon and when she picked it up Cassandra Marsland's voice came over the line. 'Lucinda? I thought you were away, but I caught a glimpse of you in the town this morning. Is everything all right?'

She could have told her that it wasn't. That everything was all wrong due to her husband, but it wouldn't be strictly true. Bevan was merely the vehicle of her conscience. . . the prodder who had made her ruin her chances with Rafe. Avoiding answering, she said, 'I'd been to see the family of one of my nurses who died a couple of days ago.'

'I see,' Cassandra replied, and there was something in her voice that made Lucinda think that it wasn't just a social call.

'Is everything all right with *you*?' she probed. 'You sound rather distracted.'

There was silence for a moment and then Cassandra said slowly, 'I'm worried about the baby, Lucinda, and I wondered if you would examine her.'

'Me?' she said in surprise. 'You mean it's something orthopaedic?'

'Yes.'

'What is it?'

'I'll discuss it when I see you,' Cassandra said in a low voice. 'Bevan has just come in.'

'And obviously he's not going to approve of my examining Imogen?' she said drily.

'When can you see her?' Cassandra asked, ignoring the comment.

'It's up to you,' she told Cassandra. 'I'm back on the job next week, so it can either be at the Infirmary or when I come to Springfield to check on my post-operatives... or you could bring her here today for a cursory examination, but I would prefer to see the baby with all my equipment to hand.'

'I think the Infirmary,' the anxious mother said. 'For one thing Bevan is buzzing about a lot of the time at Springfield.'

'I'm not too happy about the secrecy of all this,' Lucinda told her. 'Shouldn't he be informed about what you're planning, as I'm sure he would prefer you to take Imogen elsewhere? I'm not his most favourite person, you know, and my standing will be even lower if you involve me in something that he doesn't approve of. Is *he* of the opinion that there is an orthopaedic problem?'

'Yes, and we've had a few words about it. He wants me to take her to Bristol, but I would prefer *you* to treat Imogen, Lucinda. I've seen how you work and there's none better.'

Lucinda's mouth twisted. None better at the job... none worse at everything else. But Cassandra was waiting, and if she could do anything for her baby she would be only too happy to do it. She would be even more pleased if she could tell the mother that her fears were groundless.

'All right, then. First thing Monday morning before I start my clinic?' she suggested. 'I'll phone my secretary now and tell her what we've arranged.'

'Yes, please,' Cassandra said gratefully.

When she'd gone off the line Lucinda thought ruefully that her self-imposed exile was well and truly over. First Rafe had discovered she was back. Then there had been Anne Tavistock's family to be visited. Cassandra had seen her in the town, Jake knew she'd returned, and now so would the efficient Monica, but what did it matter?

She'd admitted to Rafe that she'd come back because of him, yet except for the strange look on his face he'd taken no action. . .made no comment. The situation hadn't changed.

Lucinda saw nothing of him during the last weekend of her vacation. She wasn't expecting to. It had been merely coincidence when they'd met the other day. Although she still couldn't understand what he'd been doing on the street outside her flat. It was not on his way to the Infirmary, or the hospice where his mother was.

But the fact remained that he'd been there and had been interested enough to come up to check that all was well when he'd seen the lights on. The memory of being in his arms again was so clear that it made all that had happened since seem blurred.

However, on Monday morning there was nothing blurred about the amount of work that had accumulated during her absence, and as Monica brought her up to date with all that had gone on Lucinda was preparing herself for the fray.

But first there was Cassandra and baby Imogen to see, and she wasn't exactly looking forward to that. . .not with an uninformed Bevan in the background.

'So what's the problem, Cassandra?' she asked as a sister

showed mother and baby into her room in the consultancy suite.

'If I lie Imogen face downwards when she's undressed, the lower part of her spine seems to curve to the left,' Cassandra said, going straight to the point. 'She seems to be able to move her limbs satisfactorily, and her neck and head, but there's something not quite right, Lucinda.'

'And you say that Bevan is of the same opinion?'

'Yes, he is.'

'Right,' Lucinda said decisively, with a smile for the sleeping cherub who was shortly going to be disturbed. 'We'll have a look, then. Will you take Imogen's clothes off and lay her on the bed.'

There was silence in the room as she examined the baby, with Cassandra's anxiety a tangible thing in the atmosphere. When she'd finished Lucinda knew that what she had to say wasn't going to diminish it.

'You are right,' she told her. 'There is a lateral angulation of the spine. It might be scoliosis. . .infantile idiopathic structural scoliosis. . .but before we start jumping to conclusions Imogen needs to be X-rayed.'

'It isn't congenital or neurological, is it?' Cassandra asked with her voice full of dread. 'I've never come across it. Although I suppose I should know something about it, being a nurse.'

'There are so many malfunctions of the spine,' Lucinda said reassuringly. '*I'm* the one who is supposed to have all the info on them at my fingertips, not you, and with regard to your question the answer is no, not usually. There is no known cause. But let's get the plates done first and then we'll know better.'

By this time Imogen was howling lustily. Lucinda commented drily that there was obviously nothing wrong with her lungs, but Cassandra couldn't dredge up a smile.

'It isn't easy to X-ray a child of Imogen's tender years for this sort of thing,' Lucinda remarked, 'as she can't stand up. But the radiologist will take the pictures in a position where the angle of the baby's most prominent rib is projected across the spine. It's the amount of projection that's the important thing. No doubt while all that is being done your little miss will be expressing her disapproval.

'When you've been to Radiology, go and have a cup of tea, Cassandra, and I'll send my secretary to find you when we have the X-ray results back.' She gave Cassandra's hand a quick squeeze, 'And don't worry. Whatever your husband may think of me, I *do* know my job.'

'He knows that beyond any doubt,' Cassandra said earnestly. 'And if he had any misgivings, he has only to observe the excellent work you've done on the hordes of your patients who go to Springfield for after-care. Your name is a byword there.'

Lucinda laughed. 'Rafe Davidson calls me Beckman the Bone Woman.'

Cassandra eyed her in surprise. 'Does he really? Are you *that* close? And that reminds me. Why did you rush off from the party we gave for him? I thought you said that you were his guest.'

'Yes, I was, but there was something I'd forgotten.'

She wondered what Cassandra would say if she were to tell her that the thing she'd overlooked was her husband's animosity. But she hadn't overlooked it, had she? She'd remembered it very well, but had let Rafe coax her into going alone and leaving herself wide open to Bevan's taunts.

*   *   *

The X-rays showed that Imogen *was* suffering from scoliosis, and because the curve had shown a progression to over thirty degrees Lucinda told her, 'I will have to instigate treatment, I'm afraid, Cassandra.'

'What kind?' she asked chokingly.

'A simple plaster cast to hold the little one's spine straight. She will need to wear it for some months but hopefully it will do the trick. Most infants develop straight spines once the problem has been dealt with, so try not to distress yourself too much.'

'Thank goodness it's winter,' Cassandra said glumly. 'I'd hate Imogen to be cooped up in something like that in hot weather.'

'What are you going to tell Bevan?' Lucinda asked warily. 'He'll have to know.'

'Yes, of course, and he'll be frantic. He was married before, you know, and lost his wife and small son in an air crash. If anything happened to Imogen. . .or Mark. . . he would go insane.'

'Nothing is going to happen to the baby,' Lucinda told her firmly, 'except that she is going to be treated for something that is not life-threatening and can be corrected. When you tell him what it is, and I'd like to bet that he's already got a pretty good idea, he'll know that there's no need to panic. Unless he sees my being involved as just cause for alarm.

'And now, if you'll take Imogen along to the plaster room, I'll give them instructions with regard to what I want done, and I shall want to see her for regular checks. Monica will make you a series of appointments.'

Cassandra turned at the door with the now sleeping baby in her arms. 'Thanks, Lucinda. I knew you would sort it out.'

'Mmm, but I didn't have any good news for you, did I?' she said ruefully.

'That isn't your fault,' Cassandra replied. 'I'd have been surprised if you'd said there was nothing wrong.'

'Maternal instinct?' Lucinda questioned with a smile, and she wondered if *she* would ever experience it.

Her first day back had been long and tiring, and by half past eight she had showered and changed into silk pyjamas and a matching robe with the intention of going to bed as soon as she'd eaten.

But her plans were interrupted by the buzzer at her door. When she opened it Rafe was standing there, haggard and unshaven, dressed in a leather jacket and jeans and with a crash helmet dangling from his hand.

'Can I come in?' he asked tonelessly.

She stepped back. 'Yes, of course.' Something was telling her not to question him, and so she said easily, 'Go and sit near the fire. It's a cold night to be out on the bike. Can I make you a drink? Hot chocolate or a whisky, maybe?'

He ignored the offer and said raggedly, 'She's gone, Lucinda. . .half past four this afternoon.'

She went across and took his cold hand as he sat hunched by the fire. 'I'm so sorry. . .so very sorry,' she told him, squatting at his feet. 'I only met your mother once but I thought her a lovely person. She wouldn't want any of you to grieve. "Do you not think that you should be with your father and Zoe and young Miles?' she asked carefully as she tried not to surmise about what had brought him to *her* on such a day.

Rafe shook his head. 'I haven't deserted them. I only came here briefly. I needed to be with someone who isn't family for a short time. It may sound strange, but that is how I felt.'

He laid his head back against the chair and closed his eyes. 'We were all prepared for it, but it doesn't hurt any less, Lucinda. For the last few months this day has been looming over me like a black cloud, and now that it has finally come I'm numb with pain. . .and relief.'

'Have you been at the hospice ever since we met last week?' she asked.

'Mmm,' he answered wearily, 'apart from dashing home to shower and change once in a while.'

'You must be exhausted,'

He shrugged. 'I'm all right. When Bevan and I were out in Bosnia we slept when and if we could, and after a few months of that one *can* do without—or, if the situation demands it, sleep on a clothesline.'

Lucinda released his hand reluctantly and got to her feet. 'Let me make you a drink?'

'Yes, I'd like that. My throat's dry as a bone.' He gave a weary smile. 'Sorry about the bone bit. You've been back in harness today, I suppose.'

'You could say that,' she agreed, and padded off into the kitchen to make the drink she had promised him. He hadn't stated any preference and, not being too happy about his distressed state, she passed over the whisky and went for the hot chocolate.

By the time she went back into the lounge with a steaming mug, Rafe was slumped in the chair in an exhausted sleep.

After the first few moments she went to phone his family. If they were needing him desperately she would have to awaken him, but she was loath to do it. This was clearly the first sleep he'd had in days and it would be a shame to break into it if it wasn't necessary.

His father answered, and after she had expressed her sorrow on their behalf she explained that Rafe was at her flat and fast asleep.

'Don't disturb him,' Albert Davidson said immediately. 'Rafe has carried the burden for us all. Without him we wouldn't have survived. He is the one who has lost the most sleep, and now that there is no longer anyone to watch over, let him rest. I thought that he might have gone to your place, my dear. I think that his mother had hoped that the two of you. . .'

His voice trailed away as she goggled at the receiver in amazement, and when he discovered that she had no comment to make Rafe's father wished her a constrained goodbye.

CHAPTER SIX

THE hours passed and still he slept. As Lucinda feasted her eyes on the mobile face that was lost and defenceless in sleep, she marvelled that it was this man above all others who had brought warmth and softness to her heart.

Not a slick man of the world, or a sensual smoulderer, but a man who cared deeply for his folks, had an easy manner, was soon given to laughter.

But hidden beneath those facets of his character was a strength of mind and an idealism that had forced her to admit to herself that she'd been mistaken to class him as lightweight. There were depths to him that made her own character seem shallow in the extreme.

Sadly for her, it was this same man who had found her wanting, and yet, amazingly, it was here that he had come in his hour of need.

Let that mean something, she prayed. Don't let me be just any old port in a storm.

His hand was hanging loosely over the arm of the chair and she took it and held it to her cheek. His fingers tightened around hers and she thought contentedly that he knew she was there.

On that presumption she too slept, until she was awakened by a groan, and as her eyes flew open she saw that Rafe was awake, looking down on her joylessly as she crouched beside the chair.

'It's true, isn't it?' he said flatly. 'I haven't dreamt it. She's gone!'

'Yes, your mother has died, Rafe,' she said softly. 'You didn't dream it. You came here to tell me. . .and fell asleep from exhaustion.'

He turned his head away but she knew there would be no tears. Victoria had made a pact with her family. . .that they had to get on with their lives. . .there must be no grieving. It would be a betrayal of her valiant spirit if he let her down, but it didn't stop him from turning back to her and saying desperately, 'Hold me, Lucinda. Help me to forget for a few seconds.'

She opened her arms and incredibly he went into them as if he belonged there. Reaching up, she pressed her lips against his brow, his closed lids, and on the rough stubble of his cheek, finally brushing his mouth with the gentlest of kisses.

There had never been a less likely moment for passion, but for some reason it was there, and as her lips drew away from his Rafe claimed them again with a desperate sort of urgency. Because she couldn't help herself Lucinda responded to him, even though she knew that it was grief that was driving him.

'Comfort him for me,' Victoria's voice seemed to say from far away. . .and comfort him she did. With her mouth, her voice, murmuring words of endearment—and her body, responding to his hunger with a tenderness that she would never have believed herself capable of.

Lucinda knew that if they continued like this it was inevitable that they would make love, but something held her back. If ever that happened it must be for the right reasons, not because he was disorientated with grief. Reluctantly, she eased herself out of his arms.

'What's wrong?' he asked thickly.

'Nothing,' she told him quietly, 'except that if we go

on from here you won't be able to live with yourself tomorrow. Go home, Rafe. Your family need you.'

'And *you* don't?'

The bleak statement hurt like the turning of a knife and she gave him a push in the direction of the door. 'Don't put words into my mouth. Just go, and I'll forget you said that.'

He put his hand to his brow as if his thought processes were beginning to function once more. 'I must be insane to behave like this with my mother dead only a few hours,' he said flatly, and, shaking his head in disbelief, he went.

Having him in her home and in her arms again had been magical, but during what was left of the night Lucinda faced up to the certainty that she *had* been the port in the storm he had sought. She wondered if, when Rafe was calmer, he would recall that it was *she* who had resisted him, had refused to take advantage of his grief.

She hoped so, as she was short on Brownie points as far as their relationship went—if one could call it that. She supposed that tonight could have been an opportunity to take it a step further, but there was no way she was going to accept second best with this man.

If he continued to reject her, then so be it. She was not lacking in principles.

His father's remark on the phone earlier kept coming back to mind, and her amazement was undiminished as she tried to take in the fact that Victoria had thought there was something between Rafe and herself.

But, of course, on the night he'd taken her to visit his mother there *had* been. With another woman's perception Victoria must have seen the beginning of an attraction between them, and wouldn't have known that shortly afterwards it had fizzled out on Rafe's part because of her own shortcomings and Bevan Marsland's unabated censure.

The next day she was tired and irritable, and Monica asked warily, 'Is anything wrong, Dr Beckman?'

Lucinda eyed her absently, pushing to the back of her mind mesmerising pictures of the night before

'No,' she fibbed. 'I'm just a bit on edge, that's all.'

'I believe that Dr Davidson has lost his mother,' the other woman probed tactfully, and Lucinda nodded morosely.

'Yes. That is so,' she said briefly. If Monica was fishing for information there was no way it was going to come from her, but it seemed as if it was to be the other way round.

'The family live quite near me,' her secretary said. 'They're charming people. Mrs Davidson used to be a singer. She had a lovely voice. I've heard her sing on TV and in variety shows in the area, and her husband was mayor a couple of years back.'

'Really?' It was Lucinda's turn to throw a line. 'And Rafe—Dr Davidson—what do you know about him?'

Monica thought for a moment. 'Not a lot. I remember him being offered a plum job in cardiac surgery a few years ago and he turned it down to go out to Bosnia. He's very well thought of in medical circles. He has all the same skills as Sir Thomas but with a much more enlightened outlook, yet it didn't prevent him risking life and limb out there.'

'Yes, I know he's been in Bosnia,' Lucinda said. 'That's where he met Bevan Marsland, one of the GPs on call at Springfield.'

'Rafe Davidson's always had the women after him,' Monica said with a smile. 'But the only time I can recall him succumbing was when he became engaged to Justine Simmons just before he went away.'

Lucinda was eyeing her in amazement. 'You're not referring to a relative of our esteemed Sir Thomas?'

Monica nodded. 'The old boy's daughter, no less.'

'Really! And where is she now?' she spluttered.

'Wouldn't wait for him. Didn't want him to go out there to help the poor suffering victims. Rafe Davidson put his career on hold to go to Bosnia and his reward was being thrown over by a selfish little madam who'd always had her own way and couldn't believe that he could bear to leave her.'

'He wasn't exactly planning a pleasure trip, was he?' Lucinda remarked drily. 'The guy was willing to give up his time and energies for the less fortunate and she was peeved about it! The mind boggles! I can see now why he once remarked that he and Sir Tom were friends of long standing. The old fellow might have been his father-in-law if things had worked out.'

'What happened to the girl?' she asked casually, having no wish to let Monica see just how interested she was in Rafe's past and yet unable to help herself.

'Married a wealthy Canadian and went to live over there.'

'What was she like?'

'Stunning blonde, very curvy, large amethyst-blue eyes—and a mind like a cash register,' Monica said waspishly.

'I see,' Lucinda murmured. In other words completely opposite to herself. *Her* hair was black as ebony, her eyes the dark brown that went with the colouring, her body slender rather than curving. . .and when it came to money, she was generous to a fault.

All this made it clear that any previous interest Rafe had shown in herself was certainly not because he sought a replica of the woman that he'd once been engaged to. . . who'd only cared about her own needs and motivations.

Lucinda had often thought of pulling up her own roots and offering her skills to a less fortunate country, and maybe one day she would. As things were at present she had no ties to bind her. Jake had his Melanie, and there was no likelihood of Rafe Davidson throwing a wobbly if she disappeared from the scene, as he'd already decided that she was flawed goods. Perhaps it *was* time she moved on to pastures new.

She went to Springfield later that afternoon, and as she was checking on her patients Bevan Marsland appeared at her side.

The mere fact of him seeking her out was an event in itself, and when he asked if she could spare a moment Lucinda found herself tensing. Was this going to be another taking to task session because he'd found out that Cassandra had asked her to treat Imogen?

'What can I do for you?' she asked coolly when they went outside on the corridor.

'I think you've already done it,' he said levelly.

So she'd been right. He wasn't pleased. But what was new about that? And yet what was it that he was saying? Her eyes flew open as it registered.

'I just wanted to thank you for what you've done for Imogen,' he said stiffly. 'As you may be aware, I was a paediatrician before I took over the village practice, and I had a pretty good idea what was wrong, but it is never advisable to try to diagnose one's own family.'

He gave a reluctant smile. 'As Cassie keeps telling me,

we needed the best for Imogen's problem. . .and I think we are both agreed that you're it.'

Relief was flooding through her in a welcoming tide. Was this the end of his antagonism. . .? Being who she was, she had to ask. . .

'Does this mean that we can be friends at last?' she asked carefully.

He eyed her sombrely. 'Yes. I suppose so. I've grieved over Darren long enough, and nothing either of us can do will bring him back.'

'No,' she agreed quietly, 'and I've lived with remorse for a long time. It has affected my life, and helped to make me what I am.'

He held out his hand and said, 'I'm sorry, Lucinda. I should have shown more tolerance.'

It was an emotional moment, and to lighten it she said, 'Maybe you could tell your friend, Rafe, that we've healed the rift? I told him about what happened long ago and *he* took a dim view of it, too.'

'And does that matter?' he asked curiously.

It mattered all right, mattered a lot, but she wasn't going to admit it. . .not 'Beckman the Bone Woman', who was supposed to be as hard as nails, and so she said easily, 'No, not really. It was just a passing thought.'

Rafe came back on duty the following week. Lucinda had only seen him once since the night that he'd slept in her apartment, and that had been from a distance as she'd hovered at the church gate for a few seconds, watching his mother's funeral take place.

She hadn't gone inside for the service as she'd been due in Theatre in half an hour. Even if she hadn't been, she would have hesitated to intrude on the famliy's grief, but the need to see him, if only for a second, had been strong. As his mother's body had been carried into the church she had hurried back to the hospital under a pale winter sun.

On his first morning back she didn't get the chance to speak to him. Sir Thomas was fussing and expostulating when she passed them in the corridor and she thought indignantly that he was about as insensitive as his daughter, if Monica's description of her could be relied upon.

Why couldn't he lay off for a while, give his second-in-command time to get his breath? But Rafe was coping in his usual easy manner. Only the fact that he was thinner, and there were shadows beneath his eyes, told her that he was stressed.

But whereas she was prone to explode under stress he was totally calm. As calm as he'd been on the day when he'd told her there was no likelihood of their lives ever being intertwined.

He came to find her at lunchtime, leaning against the doorjamb of her office. When she lifted her head and their eyes met, he said, 'Two things. I'm sorry about that night in your flat...and I thought you might have come to the funeral.'

Lucinda got to her feet and walked round the desk to stand in front of him. 'You don't need to be sorry about what happened on the night your mother died.'

He winced. 'Yes, I do. I don't know what she would have thought of me.'

'She would have understood,' she told him. '*She* had gone beyond offering you comfort...but *I* was around.' Her voice hardened at the last few words, and although she was ashamed of the fact, she couldn't help it.

If only he had come to tell her that he'd needed *her* on

that night, that she had been the only one he wanted to be with. But no. He was apologising for being with her, making them both sound guilty of something disgusting, when it had been moving and tender.

He caught the inflection in her voice and his eyes darkened. 'Yes, you *were* around. I'm not likely to forget that.'

What was that supposed to mean? she wondered. That she was better than nothing? That he was going to remember that she'd been ready and willing to let passion intrude into their sombre meeting? Maybe he felt that she'd instigated it, because hadn't she kissed him?

Yes, but it had only been a butterfly kiss. Rafe was the one who'd turned it into something else. It was time to talk about other things, she decided.

'I *did* come to church on the day of the funeral,' she told him evenly, 'but I couldn't stay. I was due in Theatre, and in any case, I didn't want to intrude.'

'You wouldn't have done. There were droves of people there, including those who'd known my mother as a singer, the children and teachers from the school where she'd taught, my father's mayoral friends, and an old acquaintance of mine who's over from Canada.'

'Really?' she said casually as her spirits took a downward plunge. 'And who would that be?'

'Sir Tom's daughter. We were engaged once.'

'So I believe.'

It wasn't in her nature to pretend that she hadn't known, but she couldn't resist a probe. 'Visiting her parents, is she?'

'That, and taking a break from a difficult husband.'

'Oh, so *you've* been offering a comforting shoulder?'

For the first time since he'd lost his mother Rafe looked like his old self as his lazy smile appeared and he said,

'Yes, it seems to be something that we're both able to provide.'

Lucinda turned away. So forgiveness was there for the asking for the blonde beauty who wouldn't wait for him, but her own transgressions hadn't been overlooked so easily. With the distinct feeling that it was going to be one of those days, she said with chilly precision, 'Yes, it does appear so, but there is something else that we both pro- vide—health care—and I've got a clinic waiting for me, so. . .'

He raised a placatory hand. 'All right, message received. Just one thing before I consider myself duly dismissed.'

'What?' she muttered, knowing that if he stayed a second longer her irritation would disappear and longing would take its place.

There was a glint of amusement in his eyes as he said, 'Sir Tom and Lady Simmons are having a welcome home party for their offspring, and, as the cast-off fiancé, I'm invited. Strangely, history seems to be repeating itself. I've been invited to bring a guest. How are you fixed?'

She glared at him. How was she fixed? She was fixed so that if he asked her to pull his sledge all the way to the North Pole she would do it. . .as long as they shared the same igloo at the end of the journey.

But did she want to feature continually in his life as a stop-gap? Of course she didn't, but for some reason, since meeting Rafe Davidson, she seemed to have lost her force- ful ways. The man with the humorous brown eyes and the heart of steel was turning her into a yes-woman.

'When is it?' she asked casually, to give herself breathing space.

'Saturday night.'

'I suppose I could manage it, although I don't normally mix with the likes of Sir Tom and his friends. But if *you're* going to be tagging along with the prodigal daughter. . .'

'I won't be doing that,' he assured her, suddenly serious, and as her world righted itself to some extent, he knocked it off its axle once more. 'Justine is still married.'

'And, of course, you're a man of honour,' she commented caustically.

He didn't rise to the bait, just stood gazing at her as if she were some sort of puzzling specimen that he hadn't encountered before. Then to her annoyance he said, 'You won't go running off like you did last time?'

'You know why I did that!' she snapped. 'Your friend Bevan was making his snide remarks. But there has been a truce. I have been of some use to him, and because of it he has decided to pardon my youthful sins.'

Her meeting with Bevan Marsland hadn't really been like that, and she was ashamed of how she was describing it, but the desire to hit out at Rafe was strong. . .and all because of his swings from indifference to interest.

'And what was it that you were able to do for him?' he asked immediately.

'I was able to treat his little daughter to his satisfaction.'

'Imogen?'

'Well, yes. He hasn't got any other daughters that I'm aware of.'

He ignored the sarcasm. 'What's wrong with the baby?'

'Scoliosis.'

He frowned. 'That's not good.'

'No, it isn't,' she agreed, still on the defensive, 'but I have it under control.'

He sighed. 'Yes, of course. You will have. They reckon

your department is the most efficient in the place.'

'What about Sir Tom and yourself?' she asked, resisting the temptation to tell him that until recently the job had been the only thing that mattered in her life. 'I'm told that your unit works to a very impressive standard.'

'It might be even more impressive if he would let me have more flexibility. Do you know, I can almost believe that he was relieved we didn't end up getting involved with the heart shrink surgery for your colleague, Anne Tavistock.'

'If that's the case he should be ashamed,' she said angrily. 'We are honour bound to do what we can to improve the quality of life for our patients.'

'And what about the quality of life of we doctors?' he said laughingly.

She almost groaned. 'What about it?'

'Nothing. It was just a joke.'

The quality of *her* life *was* a joke, she thought soberly, and it didn't look like improving at the present time if the best Rafe could do was invite her to a party as his hanger-on.

His nearness was a constant temptation and she began to walk away from him, moving towards her desk, but he took her arm and pulled her gently back towards him.

'So you'll come on Saturday, then?'

'I've said I will.'

His touch was magic, his nearness a delight, and if he'd started to make passionate love to her there and then in the office she wouldn't have resisted. But he merely chucked her under the chin and said calmly, 'Until Saturday, then.'

When he'd gone she sat deep in thought. What had she let herself in for? A boring evening with the Simmons family and their cronies? But it wouldn't be boring with Rafe around, would it...and the curvy Justine!

During that week Jake rang one evening to say that he and Melanie would be in the Infirmary on the Friday. They'd told the young mother-to-be at the antenatal clinic that she had a heart murmur and had made her an appointment to see a cardiac specialist.

Jake sounded worried, and, although she wasn't too happy about it herself, Lucinda assured him that pregnancy could bring on that sort of thing in instances where the pregnant woman had never before had any problems, and that it often cleared up after the birth.

'We'll call in to see you while we're there,' he suggested.

Although the middle of a busy day at the hospital wasn't her idea of the best place to meet up with her brother and his girlfriend, she knew that it would be the quickest way of finding out what the verdict was on Melanie's heart murmur.

A patient of her own was causing her some concern at the present time too. Suzy Cheung's father owned a res-taurant on the outskirts of the town, and the pretty Chinese girl had been sent to the orthopaedic unit by her GP.

She was suffering from severe joint pains and looked frail and ill. The first thing that Lucinda had noticed was a butterfly-shaped blotchy rash on her cheeks and the bridge of her nose, and alarm bells rang.

As well as the joint pains, the girl was suffering from fatigue, nausea and weight loss, and those factors, along with the rash, were indicative of a chronic disease with no known cure—lupus erythematosus, an illness that affected the connective tissue of the body, the material that holds its structures together.

Blood tests and a skin biopsy were carried out and confirmed Lucinda's worst fears. But as she explained the seriousness of the illness to the Chinese girl, her young patient's dismay was centred around the fact that she mightn't be able to work, rather than that her body had been attacked by an incurable disease.

'My father needs me to help in the restaurant!' she said in a panic. 'I cannot be ill. He will be angry!'

'Miss Cheung, you *are* ill,' Lucinda told her levelly. 'That is the first thing you have to accept. Although it is an illness that sometimes goes away, it is only for a short time...and it always comes back. You may need to see other doctors besides myself, with regard to your kidneys or neurological problems, amongst others, but there *is* treatment available.'

She saw no point in explaining to the almost hysterical girl that she was going to prescribe anti-inflammatory drugs for the joint pain and antimalarial treatment for the rash. Sufficient to hand her the prescription with instructions to get it made up immediately and to take the medication without fail.

'Avoid sunlight,' was her last comment as Suzy Cheung got up to go, and when the girl gazed at her blankly, Lucinda wondered if she ever saw *daylight*, let alone the sun's rays.

She was familiar with the Wang Su Chinese restaurant and take-away, and vowed that she would dine there the first chance that presented itself, to observe for herself just how her patient was progressing.

Jake and Melanie arrived at the consultancy suite just as she was going for lunch on Friday, and they ended up dining together in the hospital's cafeteria.

'And so what did the heart man have to say?' Lucinda asked in her usual direct manner once they were seated.

'That they will monitor my heart regularly during my pregnancy and that there is no cause for alarm at the moment,' Melanie said with relief in her eyes.

Rafe went past the cafeteria entrance at that moment and when he saw them there he hesitated, his eyes questioning, but Lucinda didn't call him over and after a moment he carried on to wherever he was going.

She reasoned glumly that if they *were* going to be 'ships that passed' there was no point in introducing him to *her* family. In fact she still hadn't worked out why he'd taken her to meet *his*.

At the time she'd thought she knew the answer, and had been happy and expectant about the event, but that had been before she'd told him about Darren Marsland.

He caught up with her in the hospital car park at six o'clock, and when she saw him striding towards her in his riding leathers, with the wind whipping his cheeks to a healthy glow and tousling the burnished brown pelt that would soon be obscured by his helmet, her heart began to thump unevenly.

'The blonde girl I saw you dining with at lunchtime,' he said, getting straight to the point. 'she was on my list for this morning. . .heart murmur due to pregnancy. Is she an acquaintance of yours?'

'Well, I don't usually eat with strangers,' she said irritatingly. 'She's my brother's live-in girlfriend, Melanie.'

'That was your brother you were with?' he said in slow surprise. 'Why didn't you introduce me?'

Typical, she thought. If she *had* introduced Jake he might have thought she was presuming too much, and now, because she *hadn't*, he wanted to know why.

Because she was weary of the see-sawing of her emotions, and always ready to call a spade a spade she told him. 'I didn't introduce you to my brother for two reasons. Firstly because you might have thought that I was getting too chummy, and secondly, as you were so quick to point out, our lives are not likely ever to be...what was the word you used?'

'Intertwined,' he said slowly. 'But that was because I wanted you to be...'

Sir Thomas was bearing down on them, tutting when he saw that the motorcycle was still parked beside his car, and when he said irritably, 'Are you going to move that contraption, Rafe, while I get the Jaguar out?' the rest of what Rafe had been about to say was left unsaid.

'I believe that you are joining us tomorrow night, Lucinda,' the elderly consultant said as Rafe mounted the bike.

'Er...yes. I'm looking forward to it,' she fibbed.

But then it wasn't a full fib, was it? She *wasn't* looking forward to the party, but an evening with the man who was now raising his hand in a brief salute before he zoomed off into the night was not to be sneezed at. It was the rest of the company that she was dubious about.

'You know that my daughter, Justine, is home from Canada?' Thomas Simmons said. 'The party is in her honour and she insisted that Rafe was invited because he and she were once very close.'

'Is her husband with her?' Lucinda asked, feeling as sour as the proverbial gooseberry.

'Er...no...I'm afraid not. He has been detained unavoidably,' he said uncomfortably, and without giving her the chance to question him further he slid behind the wheel of his car and drove off.

So, if nothing else, the party was going to be interesting, Lucinda thought as the Mercedes purred along behind Sir Thomas's car. Maybe it was time she made a stand, let Rafe see that she wasn't the meek push-over that she must have appeared of late.

She would get dressed up to the nines and make her own contribution to the entertainment. It was a long time since she'd done anything spectacular, and, after all, she'd nothing to lose. Even if Rafe *didn't* stir up the embers of a past relationship, he certainly wasn't carrying a torch for herself. So why not?

Driving along the high street, she saw that the shops were showing their Christmas displays. Fairy lights hung from the street lamps and there was a huge Christmas tree in the main square. Soon it would be one of the happiest seasons of the year, and as usual she would be spending it alone as Jake was never around for the festive season.

In past years her solitude had been from choice, because she'd had a chip on her shoulder and wouldn't accept invitations that came her way, telling herself that the sooner it was over the better. She'd reasoned that Christmas was a time for romance and families being together, and as neither of those things featured in her life she'd opted out.

But this year it could have been so different. She could have spent it with the man who had pierced her armour. Pierced it to such an extent that he was constantly in her thoughts.

His Christmas would be lacking a loved one this time, and, although she would never presume to think she could fill Victoria's place in his life, it would have been sweet contentment to be with him as part of his family, no longer the outsider.

As if to emphasise the fact that Christmas was indeed

on its way, when she got back to the flats the porter was
erecting the expensive spruce that always graced the foyer.
She thought grimly that all it needed now was for the
Rotary Club's sledge to pull up outside and her depression
would be complete.

CHAPTER SEVEN

THE residence of Sir Thomas and Lady Simmons was imposing in the extreme, and when Rafe pulled up outside in his most recent acquisition, a British racing green Mini-Cooper, he gave a whimsical smile.

'Sir Tom and his wife are hardly slumming it, are they?' he commented, with a quick glance at Lucinda's set profile.

The night had started off badly because of his expression when she'd opened the door of her flat to him earlier, and it had gone from bad to worse when, on seeing the Mini, she'd suggested that she drive them to the party in her Mercedes.

She'd chosen to wear a dress that had been hanging in her wardrobe for just such an occasion. Made out of vivid turquoise silk, it was low-cut at front and back with only a boned bodice for support, and showed her creamy shoulders and the smooth rise of her breasts to their best advantage.

A crystal choker necklace around her throat and long matching drops in her ears completed the effect, and her mirror told her that she looked what she was. . .a mature and beautiful woman.

Only the dark-lashed eyes gave the game away, telling the observant onlooker that mature and beautiful she might be, but happy and fulfilled she was not.

As she'd opened the door to her escort for the night his eyes had darkened in approval, but there'd been a sort of frustrated regret in his expression that had taken the fizz out of the anticipation that had been building up inside her.

'What's wrong?' she'd asked tightly.

'Nothing,' he'd replied, composing his features.

'Yes, there is,' she'd persisted. 'Don't you like my dress?'

He'd laughed, but there had been no mirth in it. 'You really don't have to ask me that. It's stunning. . .and so are you. There won't be a man there who isn't so aware of you that all the other women cease to exist.'

She had raised her eyes heavenwards. Would she ever get it right with this man? If it had been anyone else she might have thought there was jealousy behind the comment, but not with Rafe Davidson.

Because she was hurting inside, Lucinda had snapped back, 'With the exception of yourself, of course. Because *you* know that my inward attractiveness is way below any outer appeal I may have. It is fortunate that it's a party that we're going to and not a meeting of the Rechabites, otherwise I can see you having me standing up and confessing my sins!'

'Don't you think you're being rather ridiculous?' he'd said as she'd shrugged off his offer to help her into a long black silk evening coat. 'Do you always make a habit of continually dragging up casual remarks made to you in the past?'

'Casual!' she'd hissed angrily as she kissed the thought of a pleasant evening with Rafe goodbye. 'I don't recall there being anything *casual* about what you had to say when I told you about Darren Marsland. "Condemning" would be a better word.'

He'd eyed her levelly and then looked down at his watch. 'One day when we aren't so pressed for time we'll discuss that matter again. . .'

'I don't think so,' Lucinda had said glacially, 'and don't

patronise me, Rafe. I was managing my life quite well before you came along,' she'd fibbed, 'and will continue to do so.'

'All right, you've made your point,' he'd said equably, making her hackles rise even more. 'But we have to get moving, Lucinda, or the Simmons family will think that we aren't coming.'

'I've bought a car,' he'd said as she'd walked stiffly beside him down the stairs. 'A small runabout for when I don't want to use the bike.'

When she'd seen the Mini Lucinda had said grumpily, 'I've travelled in one of these before, and by the time I got out of it I thought that I was going to have to rearrange my own bones. I'd rather we used the Merc.'

She was being difficult and knew it, but Rafe had merely rubbed an appreciative hand along the metallic green bonnet and remarked, 'Not the style you're used to, eh?'

'If you mean I'm a snob,' she'd snapped, miserable after counting the minutes to seeing him again, 'I'm not. Neither do I sit in judgement on others.' On that note she'd marched up to the small green car and tucked herself in with all the elegance she could muster.

And now, as she met his enquiring glance, the mood was still upon her, and she didn't have any comment to make about the lifestyle of a doctor who had a similar status to her own, except for the fact that Thomas Simmons had been working at it longer.

Their elderly colleague and his wife were greeting the guests at the door, and when Sir Thomas saw Lucinda beside Rafe he said, 'Ah, so you *have* brought Dr Beckman. Nice to see you, my dear.'

He turned to where a tiny blonde was chatting to another guest and, drawing her towards them, he said, 'Justine, meet Lucinda—Dr Beckman.' And to Lucinda, 'This is my daughter, Justine Horrocks.' Glancing across at Rafe, he said with forced jocularity, 'I don't need to introduce *you* to Justine, do I, Rafe?'

It seemed to Lucinda at that moment as if they were all players in a drama. Sir Tom was effusive in his welcome, but his daughter gave her a brief nod and then focused all her attention on Rafe, and Lucinda thought herself the patsy. The stop-gap brought along to make things look respectable...even though she wasn't respectable herself.

It felt as if this meeting with the woman who had once been the recipient of Rafe's affections, and maybe still was, was being stage-managed. Perhaps the Canadian husband was about to be discarded, or already had been, and the Simmons daughter was making new plans. Maybe on Rafe's part he saw it as an opportunity to get the message over that their relationship wasn't going anywhere.

As the party got under way, Lucinda became aware of various things. One of them was that marriage and her life in Canada hadn't blotted out Justine Horrocks' interest in Rafe, and another was that she, Lucinda, appeared to be the only one not happy about the fact.

Her parents looked on fondly as Justine monopolised him, and he didn't seem to be making any effort to shake her off as he listened attentively to words that were for his ear alone.

Eventually, in cold anger, Lucinda allowed one of the other guests to entertain her. His name was Jack Montrose and he too was employed in health-care. He was also fair of hair and skin, like the predatory Justine, and she thought to herself that the blonds were out in full force tonight.

Jack's function was in administration, as assistant manager of the trust that controlled the hospital, and he was recently divorced, so she supposed it wasn't surprising that being foot-loose and fancy-free he'd latched on to her, the eternal bachelor woman.

They had several dances together, during which he held her far too close, and when supper was announced they sat together, gathering around them other lively souls until the noise from their part of the room was deafening.

At one point she found Rafe at her shoulder, and he hissed angrily, 'For God's sake, Lucinda! Do you have to be involved in all this racket?'

She laughed up at him, and with the devil in her said innocently, 'Why? What's the matter? Can't you hear the sweet nothings being whispered in your ear?'

'You're jumping to conclusions,' he said coldly. 'She's an old friend and the least I can do is listen to her troubles.'

'In other words you're showing her more consideration than she showed you?'

'Meaning?'

'Meaning that she married someone else while you were away doing your bit in Bosnia.'

'That was her affair.'

'So you weren't bothered?'

'Yes, of course I was,' he snapped. 'But we are all what we are, Lucinda.'

She swivelled round in her chair and glared at him. 'Really? What a tolerant person you are. You can accept the fact that your fiancée found herself another man while you were performing one of the most worthwhile tasks a doctor can be involved in, but what about me? Were you so tolerant with me? Oh, no! I was the original sinner. The Mary Magdalene cowering at the feet of the righteous one. . .and, that being so, if my behaviour tonight continues to offend you. . .tough!'

'C'mon, Lucinda,' one of the men at the table said thickly. 'Old Jack, here, is pining for your company.'

She laughed low in her throat. 'Really? Well, in that case I'm coming.' Turning away from Rafe, she said, 'My friend is just going. . .aren't you?'

'If you say so,' he said, with a smile that should have warned her of what was to come. 'But you're coming with me.' Gripping her arm, he yanked her up out of her seat.

'I'm not!' she protested in quiet fury.

'You are,' Rafe said, with the sort of restrained tolerance one would use with a disruptive child. 'And if you don't co-operate I'll sling you over my shoulder and you'll make your exit that way. So what's it to be?'

The old Lucinda would have called his bluff and dared him to carry out his threat. Even now she was sorely tempted. But the last thing she wanted bandied about the hospital was the news that Beckman and Davidson had something going. . .and that he'd forcibly carried her out of Sir Thomas's party. If that sort of thing got around, the gossips would have a field-day.

And since when did you care about gossip or making an undignified exit from a social gathering? she asked herself as she met his inflexible gaze.

The answer came back in a flash. Ever since she'd met this tantalising copper-haired man. . .because she craved his respect and longed for his affection even more, because the tenderness she felt for him made her feel weak and defenceless. She loved the muscular grace of his body, the clear, uncluttered brightness of his mind. And the solitary furrow she had ploughed over the years wasn't going to be enough any more.

'All right, you win,' she said as weariness swept over her, but there was no sign of it in her voice as she added tightly, 'But I won't forget this. You brought me here and then discarded me while you hovered around your ex-fiancée like a fascinated brown moth.'

'Say goodnight to your *friends*, Lucinda,' he said, unperturbed, 'then we'll make our excuses to the Simmons family. And when we get outside, I'll show you how much of a moth I am.'

'Huh!' she snorted disdainfully.

It was barely eleven o'clock as they made their farewells to Sir Thomas and his wife and their pouting daughter. And as they walked towards the Mini, Lucinda said tartly, 'I suppose you've arranged to go back once you've got me off your hands!'

He was opening the car door for her. 'Don't be ridiculous. Why should I do that?'

Making no attempt to get into the small passenger seat, she looked up at him, her eyes big and luminous in the slanting light from the windows of the house. 'Only you know the answer to that,' she said coldly.

'Is that so?' he said. 'Well, I'm glad I know the answer to something, because when it comes to you, there doesn't seem to be an answer. One moment I'm dazzled by you and the next destroyed.'

'Dazzled! Destroyed!' she hooted recklessly. 'You make me sound like some sort of laser beam.'

'A very apt description, and far more compelling than. . . what was it you called me?. . .a moth? I recollect promising that I would dispel that idea once we'd left the party, and I never break a promise, Lucinda.'

She swallowed hard. His voice was soft and full of unmistakable meaning. In that moment, her misery and jealousy seemed as nothing compared to the promise in his eyes and the demanding mouth about to cover hers.

As they clung together in the cold winter night they could have been statues in the spacious garden, so enraptured were they by each other, so in tune of mind and body, but, as Lucinda told herself afterwards, nothing that wonderful was meant to last, and Jack Montrose's slurred voice, asking from the doorway when he could see her again, broke the spell.

Rafe's arms dropped away, his mouth left hers, and he said with an easiness that made her groan with silent pain, 'Any time you like, I should imagine, seeing that you both have offices on the same corridor of the Infirmary.'

The drive back to her flat was silent, each of them immersed in their own thoughts, and when Lucinda spoke for the first time it was to ask stiltedly if he'd like to come in for coffee.

'No, thanks,' Rafe said immediately. 'And that is not because I'm going back to the party. Is that clear?'

'Crystal,' she said wearily, with all the fight gone out of her.

'Good, and by the way I'm going to be away for a few days. I'm attending a medical conference in London. And if I come back to find that a groove has been worn in the passage that separates your room from that of Montrose, I'll know why, won't I?'

'Yes, you will,' she agreed flatly.

He laughed. 'Cheer up, Lucinda. If it's any comfort you dazzle me far more than you destroy me.'

With that enigmatic line in farewells he left her, walking back to his car in the cold starless night.

What a fiasco the evening had been, she thought as she undressed. A mixture of misery, mortification and brief magic that had led to a very inconclusive ending.

As she lay in hot scented water in her chromium-plated bathroom, the events were going through her mind like moving pictures. Rafe's head bent attentively towards Justine Horrocks. Her parents watching with pleased smiles, as if the fact that she had a husband tucked away somewhere didn't matter. Jack Montrose all but mauling Lucinda herself as they'd danced, and then their joining up with the rowdies.

All of those things were very clear, but for some reason the most important part of the evening, when Rafe had held her in his arms on the drive outside the house, seemed blurred, like a fantasy that she'd dreamt, and she thought grimly that that described it exactly.

The barrier was still there between them. He *was* attracted to her. She could tell that. But was it just a physical thing? Mentally they didn't seem to be in tune, and because for the first time in her life she was really in love Lucinda couldn't accept one without the other.

She was woman of the world enough to know that she hadn't imagined the way Justine looked at him. It was on the cards that her marriage was over and she was ready to go back to where she'd started from. Just how willing Rafe would be to fall in with the idea Lucinda wasn't sure.

But he was supposed to be a man of honour. Would he start up a relationship with a woman who was still married, even though in the past he'd hoped to marry her himself? It would be interesting to see. So interesting that, if it did happen, her own disillusionment would be total.

She had no time to be miserable while he was away. Her workload was huge, with clinics, stints in Theatre, and visits to the community hospital whenever necessary.

Springfield, with its quieter, less fraught atmosphere,

was like a haven of peace when she went there, with Ethan Lassiter keeping his efficient hold on things and his wife Gabriella's smiling face to be seen around the wards. There was the occasional meeting with Bevan, too, and it was good to be able to talk to him without the constant feeling of being judged.

Cassandra was due to bring Imogen to see her soon, and during the visit she was hoping to find that the little plaster vest was helping the spinal problem in the way that she was expecting it to.

Lucinda had found a rapport also with Isobel Graham, the senior sister at Springfield, a quiet, brown-haired widow with pale hazel eyes that looked almost translucent compared to Rafe's warm brown orbs.

Isobel had come to live in the area on the death of her husband, and she and her two young children were staying for the time being with her parents, who ran the post office in the nearby village.

She was efficient and caring—in every way an adequate replacement for Cassandra, who had held the position before her. Lucinda, always an admirer of efficiency, was suitably impressed as she watched her carry out her duties.

'We've got a problem, Dr Beckman,' she said, when Lucinda called in at the spotless little hospital one afternoon.

'Oh, yes?'

'Mmm. One of your patients has developed a fever right out of the blue. He was doing fine until this morning, when he awoke with a high temperature and a rash.'

'Who is it? And what have you given him?' she asked immediately.

'It's Terry Robinson. He came from the Infirmary yesterday after a hip replacement, and so far I haven't given him any medication as I knew you were due to call. I thought I'd wait to see what your instructions are.'

'Sounds like an infection,' Lucinda said, already on her way to the ward.

The patient looked really ill compared to how he'd been the previous day when she'd discharged him from the Infirmary. She eyed the rash thoughtfully. There were no signs of the incision being infected, but his lymph glands were up and his eyes looked sore. 'How long have you been feeling unwell?' she asked him.

'I had a bit of a cough last week and felt nauseous, but I thought it was the after effects of the anaesthetic,' he said.

'And that is all?'

'Yes, Doctor,' he replied miserably.

'I wondered if it could be measles,' Isobel said. 'Both my children have had it and that's how it looked.'

'Measles!' Lucinda echoed. 'It seems a bit unlikely in here, and at his age.'

The retired postman was lying back with closed eyes, but he opened them at that. 'My grandson had measles the week before I was admitted to the Infirmary,' he informed them.

'It looks as if you could be right,' she told Isobel with a relieved smile. 'It certainly has the look of measles, but I didn't see how it could be that, not until he explained the connection.'

He groaned. 'I'll tell you one thing.'

'And what's that?'

'I feel a darned sight worse with this than I did after the operation.'

'Measles in an adult is a nasty thing,' she sympathised, and murmured to Isobel, who was hovering at her elbow, 'Put Mr Robinson in a darkened side ward and keep your fingers crossed that we don't have an epidemic of it in the place. Apart from that. . .'

'Bed-rest and paracetamol?' Isobel chipped in.

'Yes. . .in between exercising the hip,' Lucinda replied briskly, and went on her way.

She wasn't aware that Rafe had returned from the conference until they met in the corridor on his first morning back, and the sight of him made her heart pound in her breast.

'And so what have you been up to while I've been away?' he asked immediately as his eyes went over her trim figure in a white silk shirt and straight black trousers.

He looked down at the carpeted floor beneath their feet. 'There doesn't seem to be any extra wear and tear between your office and Jack-the-lad's. Am I to take it that the chemistry wore off once Cinderella had been dragged from the ball?'

Lucinda sighed. Typically he was treating the whole episode as a joke. It would have been far more satisfying if he'd shown jealous anger, but then he wouldn't, would he? Not if he was back in harness with Justine.

'There wasn't any chemistry,' she said evenly. 'But when one's escort is monopolised by someone else, one has to do something, hasn't one?'

It was Rafe's turn to sigh. 'I've told you, Lucinda, that I was merely offering support to an old friend. Justine has a lot of problems and needs a listening ear.'

'Yes, I remember you telling me that. I wonder why I don't believe you.'

'I don't know, but I think that we have both got better things to do than stand around discussing something that's a figment of your imagination. Let me take you out for a meal tonight to prove that what I say is true.'

'I'm already booked,' she said casually. 'I'm going to the Wang Su for a Chinese meal.'

'Who with?' he asked sharply, and if she hadn't been so keen for him to be interested in her comings and goings she might have thought that he was over-anxious to know who was taking her.

'I'm going on my own.'

'Why, for heaven's sake? I wouldn't have thought it was your sort of place. It's not in a very salubrious area for a woman on her own. You might meet up with the Triads!'

Lucinda laughed. There was pleasure inside her at his concern, and amusement at the dire consequences he was dreaming up.

'You'd better come with me, then,' she suggested teasingly.

'Yes, I will,' he agreed immediately. 'Unless you'd like to cancel the booking and I'll take you somewhere else.'

She shook her head, serious now. 'No. I have a reason for going.'

He tutted. 'What? You're going to take up Chinese cookery?'

She smiled. 'Can you see me doing that?'

'No,' he admitted. 'Martial arts, then, and you want to get the atmosphere?'

'No, again. I'm going to check on a patient.'

'What? You never cease to amaze me, Lucinda. What has one of your patients got to do with the Wang Su restaurant?'

'She works there, under the eye of what appears to be a tyrannical father. Her name is Suzy Cheung and she's got Lupus. When her condition was diagnosed she was feeling quite ill, but while I was explaining the seriousness of the disease to her she was more concerned about not being able to work in the Wang Su than her health.

'I got the impression that she's afraid of her father, and I'm going to see just how she is and what sort of a lifestyle she has there. As we both know, it's a ghastly illness and she's only a slip of a girl.'

He reached out and touched her cheek gently. 'You're a good doctor, Beckman the Bone Woman. They don't come any finer or any more dedicated.'

It was a special moment, and would have been even more memorable if he'd said that she was a fine woman in every sense. But he hadn't, and she supposed that anything was better than nothing.

'What's wrong?' he asked, as if reading her thoughts.

She shrugged. 'Just wishful thinking.' And then, throwing off her melancholy, she asked, 'So you'll come?'

'Yes. Haven't I said so? The only thing is I might be pushed for time and not able to pick you up, as I've promised to help Dad with some paperwork connected with Mum's affairs tonight, and I don't want to go back on my word. What time are you booked in for?'

'Eight-thirty.'

'I'll see you there, then. . .and Lucinda?'

'Yes?'

'Don't start falling out with the father or persuading the girl to pack in the job until I get there. Understood?'

'Yes, of course,' she agreed with deceptive mildness. 'As if I would!'

Suzy Cheung was waiting on the tables, and she recognised Lucinda the moment she walked in.

'Good evening, Doctor,' she said shyly, with an anxious

glance in the direction of the kitchen. 'I thought it was you when I saw the name on the booking.'

'How are you?' Lucinda asked in a low voice. She had already noted that Suzy looked pale and ill and seemed to be limping slightly.

'I am very well,' the Chinese girl said, avoiding her eyes. Then, as if to justify the exaggeration, she added, 'On some days I am better than on others.'

'Have you told your father about your illness?' Lucinda asked in her usual direct manner.

'Yes, and he is very sorry.'

'Sorry enough to let you give up working in this place?'

'That is not possible, Doctor.'

'Why not?'

'He cannot afford to pay someone else to do my job.'

'He would have to if you were taken into hospital?' Lucinda pointed out.

It was at that moment that Rafe arrived, and the girl took the opportunity to escape into the kitchen.

'I thought you weren't going to do anything until I got here,' he said, bringing a gust of the cold night air in with him.

'I was merely asking the girl how she's feeling,' Lucinda retaliated. 'I'm not going to create a scene. It wouldn't go down well with the directors of the hospital trust if I did.

'I'm just concerned that with the language barrier and the mania the Chinese have for working their hides off, the girl might be suffering in silence—especially if the parents have never heard of the disease. Although I would imagine that they will have, as it is more prevalent amongst their race than ours.'

Suzy kept her head down while they were ordering the food, and when she brought it to them it was the same.

She seemed to be the only one waiting on the tables. The father and any other staff were obviously occupied in the kitchen, and, short of barging in there, Lucinda couldn't see any way of holding any conversation with Suzy's father.

The place was bright and clean, the food good, and she thought that it was a pity that the small restaurant wasn't in a better part of the city. Maybe the taxes on an establishment like this were all that the Cheungs could afford.

They had finished the meal and were about to leave when the kitchen door opened and a small, wizened man came out. His hair was sparse upon his head, his eyes red-rimmed, and Rafe murmured, 'Can *this* be the tyrannical father?'

The man's eyes flicked over the smattering of diners in his modest establishment and finally came to rest on Lucinda's dark compelling looks.

His daughter had followed him out of the kitchen, and as he came across to speak to them she was at his heels. 'You are my daughter's doctor?' he asked in laboured English.

'Yes, I am,' Lucinda said evenly. 'And I am concerned about her health.'

The man nodded his head in understanding. 'You think that I am not?'

'I'm afraid that only you can answer that question, Mr Cheung, but I think that you should know there will be times when Suzy will be too ill to work, no matter how much you need her.'

He fixed her with his tired eyes. 'But not yet?'

'I can't tell you that. She is on medication, but there are so many complications with lupus.'

'Soon,' he said with a placatory note in his voice, 'soon I will get somebody in her place. My cousin will help if I pay him, but first I must have the money to do so.'

Lucinda glanced at Rafe and he smiled, as if to say, You see. Nothing is ever as bad as we expect. But she had reservations about that.

Mr Cheung was waiting to see what she had to say, and Suzy was watching with big anxious eyes. There was only one thing she could say, and she said it. 'Good. I'm pleased that you are aware of Suzy's problem. And if there is ever anything I can do to help, don't be afraid to ask.'

She picked up a handful of cards advertising the restaurant. 'One thing we can do is pass these around our people at the Infirmary, and I have a brother at the local college. I'll tell him to give them out to the students.'

The man gave a stiff little smile, and as they moved towards the door Suzy followed them. 'Thank you, Doctor. You will come again?'

'Yes, if I get the chance,' Lucinda told her. 'And don't forget I shall be wanting to see you soon for your next appointment.'

'So? Are you happy about all that?' Rafe asked when they got outside.

'Happier,' she said cautiously. 'At least the father has some idea of the seriousness of the girl's illness. I've told her that there will be periods of remission, but that the lupus will always come back in a more debilitating form.'

'I was proud of you in there,' he said, with a warmth in his eyes that she'd thought only kindled when she'd done something good medically.

She shrugged. 'It's all part of the job. You would do the same for one of your patients, wouldn't you?'

'I suppose so,' he said absently, as if his thoughts had drifted off into different waters. His gaze was still fixed on her, and in the light of the street lamps his expression seemed to have changed from friendly interest to an intensity that made her blood warm.

'What is it?' she asked huskily, as hope was born again.

'I want to hold you.'

'Why?' she asked perversely.

He groaned. 'I don't know why. It must be your amazing magnetism.'

She gritted her teeth in impatience. 'So it's not because you love me, or are desperate to be near me? I'm merely a compulsive source.'

He threw back his head and laughed. 'The word "compulsive" describes you exactly. You're in my mind far too much.'

That was a crumb she was only too eager to devour, and, unable to let the promise of the moment go, she said, 'So hold me,' and he did, cradling her to him with a seductive sort of tenderness that made feel that she'd died and gone to heaven.

Their kisses were different this time, just as passionate, just as exhilarating, but with less urgency than before, as if they both accepted that there was more stability to their relationship now. It could have gone on from there, adoring, exploring, committing, but it wasn't to be.

She drew away from him reluctantly. Hadn't she told herself countless times that there would be nothing in it for *her* unless she had his respect? So far he hadn't been bursting to tell her that he admired her integrity as well as her dedication to health-care.

'Let's go,' she said mechanically, and as he eyed her in tight puzzlement she led the way to where they'd parked their cars.

CHAPTER EIGHT

As THE countdown to Christmas took over the minds and imaginations of all those around her, Lucinda felt that the festive season was approaching far too quickly.

Christmas fever was everywhere she looked. Inside the Infirmary the wards and the hospital foyer glittered with bright baubles hanging from sturdy Christmas trees that gave off the delicious smell of pine, and in the kitchens special menus for one of the most enjoyable celebrations of the year were being concocted, so that the sick might be tempted to share in the festivities.

It was the same when she went to Springfield, and in its more rural setting the preparations there were even more attractive to the eye, as the two gardeners had extended the decorations to brightly coloured fairy lights looped around the trees in the gardens outside.

In the busy town that boasted the Infirmary, signs of the coming season were even more on view in the stores and shopping arcades, and each time she drove through it Lucinda's lack of enthusiasm increased.

Jake and Melanie were spending the Christmas period with Melanie's parents in the North, so *they* wouldn't be around to lighten her days, and she thought in a moment of maudlin self-pity that it wasn't anything new. On the rare occasions when *she* needed *Jake* he was never there.

Yet supposing he *was* going to be available? Would she want to be foisting herself on to the two young students. . . making an uncomfortable threesome? Of course not.

129

'Are you coming to the Springfield Christmas Ball, Lucinda?' Mike Drew, the newly married GP, asked casually one day when they found themselves in Ethan Lassiter's office.

'I don't know,' she said, without her usual decisiveness. 'It all depends how I'm fixed.'

She was hardly going to tell these two men that she liked and respected that her Christmas arrangements all depended on the whims of a certain cardiac consultant, who seemed to be more interested in reviving an old relationship than cementing a new one.

'I take it that *you* are both attending, with your respective partners,' she said, more for something to say than anything else.

'Yes,' Mike replied with his twinkly smile, 'if Felice and I can persuade our old nanny, Meg Jardine, to come over to mind baby Toby.'

Ethan was smiling, too, and she saw that the normally self-contained hospital manager had a buoyancy about him that she hadn't seen before.

'Yes, Gabriella and I are going,' he said. 'If all goes well *we* could be on the lookout for a babysitter ourselves, this time next year.'

'She's pregnant!' Lucinda exclaimed. 'That's wonderful!'

It was, and yet she couldn't help the feeling of envy that swamped her at the news. Everybody's lives seemed to be coming together except her own, and yet what was unusual about that? She was one of those people who made their own chaos if fate didn't create any for them.

In this instance she couldn't understand why she was being so lacking in determination. In other circumstances she would have bulldozed her way through any problems and had it sorted by now. But with Rafe and herself, something was holding her back. A kind of fear had her in its grip, fear that if she made a mess of this, she would never surface again.

Obviously it was because for the first time in her life she was really in love, and the feelings she had for him were too precious to jeopardise. If it never did come to anything, at least she wouldn't have to live with the knowledge that she was to blame for the ending of a relationship that had perished in its infancy.

In December she was surprised to get a phone call from Rafe's young sister, Zoe, and her amazement increased as the likeable blonde twenty-year-old said in her ear, 'We're having a surprise party on Saturday for Rafe. It's his birthday. Will you come?'

There was silence for a moment as Lucinda thought about it, and when she spoke her voice was guarded, concealing the pleasure that the invitation had evoked.

'Er. . .I'm not sure that he would want me there, Zoe,' she said. 'The last time he took me to a party wasn't a howling success and I haven't seen much of him lately. He seems otherwise occupied.'

'You mean the job?' Zoe questioned.

'And a certain lady.'

'Who?'

Exactly, she thought. Why in the name of heaven was she hedging? 'Justine Horrocks.'

'Surely not!' his sister expostulated. 'She played a dirty trick on him and hurt him a lot.'

'Maybe,' Lucinda conceded drily, 'but in some circumstances your brother is very forgiving.'

It was Zoe's turn to be silent, as she considered the

comment, and then she said softly, 'Do come, Lucinda. Mum would have wanted you to.'

That brought a lump to her throat. Was it possible that Victoria had approved of a hard case like herself? They'd only met the once, but, whether it was so or not, there was no way she could be so churlish as to refuse after that sort of persuasion.

'Yes, all right,' she said huskily. 'If you're sure that my being there won't ruin his night? I've been to a few parties lately and they've all been a disaster.'

'Of course it won't spoil his night!' her young prospective hostess assured her. 'We'll see you there, then.'

When Zoe had gone off the line Lucinda sat deep in thought. It was a strange request. Since the night she and Rafe had dined at the Wang Su and ended up in each other's arms again they had only seen each other briefly around the hospital, and although their meetings had been friendly enough there was something in his manner that told her he wasn't at ease with her.

Perhaps he still hadn't forgiven her for breaking up that special moment they'd shared outside the Chinese restaurant. Maybe he thought that was how she was... blowing hot and cold all the time...when in truth it was *he* who was the unpredictable one.

Little did he know that every moment spent with him, whether passionate or not, was engraved in her memory, and, sadly, one of the clearest pictures was that of he and Justine absorbed in each other.

That night she stopped off in the town on her way home and went to look for a birthday gift for him. There were countless expensive, intimate things that she would have liked to have bought if things had been how she wanted them to be between them, but she dragged herself away from gold signet rings and designer clothes and contented herself with a miniature model of the same BMW bike as his and a flask of a new aftershave appropriately named Enigma.

Typically of the way life tended to mess up arrangements, Lucinda was called back to the Infirmary late on Saturday afternoon to deal with a series of broken bones suffered by passengers in a coach pile-up, and by the time she and the rest of her team had treated the various fractures it was almost eight o'clock.

As she took off her theatre greens she pushed a strand of dark hair off her brow and sighed. The party would be starting in an hour, and in that time she had to get back to the flat, shower, change, and drive to the Davidson house in time to witness Rafe's surprise.

After moving with all speed, she was ready with time to spare, and as it was only a five-minute drive to where he lived she made herself a quick cup of tea and went to sit on the couch before the fire while she drank it.

What would he say when he saw her there? she wondered. Would he be pleased? Uncomfortable, maybe? Or dismayed? Whatever emotion he displayed, nothing would diminish *her* pleasure in being there, she thought determinedly, and her eyes misted as she remembered how Zoe had said that her mother would have wanted her to be present.

Her mouth twisted. Would Victoria have been so keen for her to be part of Rafe's life if she'd known what she was really like? She doubted it.

As she wrapped the rose cashmere coat around her and picked up the bag with the presents in it, Lucinda was having a change of heart. She would be like a fish out of water amongst the devoted Davidsons and their friends, but she'd told young Zoe she would go and so she sallied forth into the December night.

'Where *is* Rafe?' she asked as Zoe took her coat and her father offered her a sherry.

'I don't know,' the girl said, 'but he said he would be in by nine o'clock to have a couple of hours by himself. He thinks that we're all going to be out.'

The room was full, but apart from his family there was no one that Lucinda knew. They were mostly friends and neighbours and a couple of doctors from the cardiac unit.

There was no sign of Sir Thomas, and she breathed a sigh of relief to see that he was absent. The fiasco at his house was still fresh in her mind, and ever since that night she'd steered clear of Jack Montrose.

Tonight would be different, she promised herself. Here, in the friendly atmosphere of his home, their relationship might put down some roots. When she heard his key in the lock and his father whipped the light out of its socket to conceal their presence, her mood was brightening with every second.

She heard him try the switch and say, 'Strange! We seem to have an electrical fault,' and then, as the bulb was replaced and the room flooded with light once more, shrieks of 'Happy birthday!' filled the air, her own voice amongst them.

That was until she saw that he wasn't alone. Justine was clinging to his arm like a limpet and eyeing them all with annoyed china-blue eyes.

Lucinda felt sick. So much for all her hopes and aspirations. But Rafe's mouth was curving in delighted laughter, the dark hazel eyes dancing with pleasure, and if she hadn't been feeling so let down at the sight of his companion she might have thought that his gaze had gone straight to her when the lights came back on.

People were crowding around him, shaking his hand and offering their gifts, but she stood alone to one side, proud and erect, with a smile on her face that felt as if it had been painted on.

He might be charming, honourable, devastatingly attractive, she thought dismally, but he could be plausible, too. . . and manipulative. . .and if he thought that she was going to be taken in again by the story about sharing an old friend's troubles, he was very much mistaken.

'Hello, Lucinda,' his voice said at her elbow. 'Thanks for coming to my party.'

'It would have been difficult to refuse,' she said stiffly. 'Zoe can be very persuasive, and. . .'

'We Davidsons are all the same,' he murmured.

She was recovering her poise and continued blandly, 'Yes, I've noticed, but if you will let me finish. . .I was about to say that when she told me that your mother would have wanted me to be here. . .what could I say?'

'But somehow I don't think Victoria was ever aware that your ex-fiancée was back in town. Otherwise I don't think she would have considered me as a suitable partner for you.'

He reached out and gripped the hand that held the gifts. And for once his good humour was missing. 'Listen to me, Lucinda! Much as I adored my mother, I think that *I* am the one to decide who I want to be with. . .to spend my life with.'

She shrugged, as if the matter was of little concern. 'From where I'm standing, it looks as if you've already made that decision.' Thrusting the presents at him, she eased herself from his grip and said coolly, 'Happy birthday, Rafe.'

As her lips brushed his cheek she felt him tense and had the satisfaction of knowing that she could still set him on fire, in spite of Sir Thomas's daughter watching them like a hawk.

'Thanks, Lucinda,' he muttered, 'and for God's sake stop judging every sausage by its skin!'

'I'm sorry,' Zoe whispered as she and Lucinda brought the food in from the kitchen. 'I'd no idea that Rafe was going to turn up with Justine Horrocks. We'd all said that we were going out, to put him off the scent about the party, and he must have decided to bring her back here so they could be alone.'

Two minds with but a single thought, Lucinda told herself grimly, and it wasn't a happy one. If it hadn't been for the fiasco of the two previous parties she'd gone to, connected with Rafe, she would have departed once she'd given him her gift.

But it would be turning her meagre social life into a farce if she did that, so she stuck it out, her husky laugh rising above the noise, her striking face paler than usual and completely expressionless whenever Rafe came near her.

Considering that he was supposed to be with Justine, that was much more frequently than she would have expected. But each time he tried to talk to her she turned away and gave her attention to whoever was nearest, all the time knowing that she was being childish because he was free to be with whoever he wished.

You might be a force to be reckoned with at the Infirmary, she told herself glumly, but in the romance stakes you're nothing!

When it was time to go she breathed a sigh of relief. Soon, very soon, she could go home and be miserable in peace, without a pair of questioning brown eyes searching her face all the time, and equally speculative blue ones assessing her damage potential.

Maybe the next gathering she attended would require a wedding present, she thought dolefully, as she slid between the sheets of her solitary bed, but that wasn't likely to happen, was it? There was no way in a thousand years that she would go to his wedding.

Apart from the fact that it would be like cutting her own throat, did she want to see him promising to cherish a woman who hadn't loved him enough once and might be using him as a sop to her vanity a second time? He was just too good to be true.

She thought back to how he'd tried to get her alone during party without success and finally, frowning with frustration, had left her alone.

Lucinda had guessed what he wanted to say. He'd wanted to justify himself for bringing Justine back to the house when he'd thought there would be no one there, and there had been grim amusement in her to think of the shock he must have had to find them all waiting for him.

But he didn't *have* to explain, did he? She wasn't the cuckolded wife or deceived fiancée. She was merely a kissing acquaintance...around for the use of.

And that was what she pointed out to him when he buttonholed her on the hospital corridor on the Monday morning after the party.

'So you're not interested in my reasons for being with Justine?' he said soberly.

'Right in one,' she told him casually. 'You don't owe me anything.' Except my sanity and a good night's sleep!

His face had lost some of its healthy colour and his eyes were guarded as he said, 'I see. Obviously I've been under the wrong impression. I thought if we had nothing else we at least had a mutual respect for each other.'

Her dark eyes flashed. 'Respect!' she hooted. 'When I told you about my past sins you couldn't wait to tell me that you didn't want me in your life. There was no *respect* in you then, but now that *you're* seen to be less truthful than you'd like, it's a different story, isn't it? *I'm* supposed to put up with your fabrications without alluding to such things as feet of clay and forked tongues!'

'And that's how you feel about us?' he said flatly, digging deeper into her wounds.

'Us!' she hissed. 'There is no *us*, Rafe. Maybe in another time or another place there could have been, but not now . . . it's spoilt. And you're the one who's spoilt it.' On that dismal note she strode past him into her office and shut the door none too gently behind her.

Monica put in an appearance a few seconds later and said laughingly, 'I've just been telling Dr Davidson that his aftershave is dreamy, and he tells me that it was a birthday gift from an absent friend.'

Absent friend! He made it sound so sad, but what he'd said was true. She *was* absenting herself from him, and he'd only himself to blame.

Their paths didn't cross again until the Friday of that week, when she saw him coming out of Casualty looking tired and strained. Unable to help herself, she said stiltedly, 'Is everything all right?'

'Yes,' he replied, with a distinct lack of his usual sang-froid. 'If you can call having just lost a patient with a fatal arrhythmia all right.'

Lucinda eyed him levelly. 'Distressing, yes, but you must have seen it happen dozens of times in your career.'

'Of course I have,' he said with weary patience, 'but it doesn't ever get any easier. Especially when the deceased is a young impoverished mother using a grotty old iron.'

'Electrical shock?'

'Mmm. The paramedics started cardiopulmonary resuscitation in the ambulance, but there had been no pulse or breathing for ten minutes before they got to her. I injected adrenaline directly into the heart but the damage was too extensive to get it going again.'

There was no constraint between them at that moment. Their profession was the bond, and she said impulsively, 'Come into the office for a coffee. Monica always has the percolator bubbling away.'

Her secretary had gone home and there was just the two of them as he leaned back on a comfortable chair and drank the steaming liquid.

'What have you got planned for Christmas?' he asked casually as he put down the empty cup.

'Plenty,' she told him airily, and it was true up to a point. Earlier in that same day she had decided where she was going to spend the holiday period—and she wasn't referring to a round of parties or suchlike. She could imagine how his face would look were she to go into detail about her plans for Christmas and early January.

'I see,' he said flatly. 'So it's no use my inviting you out?'

'You mean as a threesome?' she asked innocently. 'You, me and Justine?'

'No,' he said, with a glint in his eyes that promised some sort of retaliation. 'Just the two of us.'

'I don't think so, Rafe. We've been into all that and I

think I might find it too strenuous trying to live up to your standards all the time.'

'For God's sake, Lucinda!' he hissed. 'Will you stop throwing that back at me? What I said that day when you told me about the business with Bevan's brother was purely a reflex comment. I couldn't bear the thought of you—'

'I've already told you that I want to put it behind me,' she interrupted coldly. 'And if you've finished your coffee. . .'

He got to his feet. 'I'd better be going. Is that what you're saying? Because if you are, I'll do just that, and while you're at it, my lovely Lucinda, you can delegate this to the past as well!' Taking her unawares, he swung her off her feet and kissed her long and thoroughly on the mouth.

It went without saying that she responded. She could handle her feelings for Rafe as long as he didn't touch her, but the moment their bodies connected she was lost, and so she kissed him back with equal passion until it seemed as if they were fused together in a tumult of sensual longing.

If a discreet cough from the doorway hadn't heralded the approach of a young nurse from the unit there was no telling where it would have led.

He stood at the opposite end of the room while Lucinda dealt with the girl's query, and when she'd gone he said, with a return to his normal equilibrium, 'So put *that* in the archives. . . If you can!'

And, with his white coat flapping against her skirt as he went past, he departed.

Now the days were flying. The excitement was building up everywhere she turned, and Lucinda felt that she must be the only person around who wasn't looking forward to the festivities. Although there *was* one other person amongst the senior hospital staff who didn't seem very happy, and it wasn't Rafe.

Whenever she saw *him* be was displaying his usual good humour, and she thought glumly that the rift between them didn't seem to be causing any gloom in that direction.

But his senior colleague didn't seem to be as full of the Christmas spirit as the rest of them, and Lucinda thought wryly that she'd never expected to see the day when she and Sir Thomas had something in common.

Whatever it was that was troubling him, he was unusually subdued. His patronising joviality was missing and he seemed to have changed from a fine elderly man into a shuffling geriatric.

Maybe he was ill, or having financial problems, or. . .a sudden thought struck her. . .experiencing daughter problems! Having met the offspring in question, Lucinda found *that* easy enough to believe. But was that likely, with such an admirable suitor hovering around his little darling?

She came across Rafe and Justine in the gloom of the hospital car park one night, and when she saw how his arm was protectively around the other woman's shoulders anger ripped through her.

What did he think he was playing at? If it wasn't for scenes like this Lucinda would have sworn that he loved Lucinda herself as she loved him, but it seemed as if he merely saw her as someone just to have fun with.

As she slid behind the wheel of the Mercedes the word had mocked her. Fun! She didn't even know the meaning of it!

Melanie was almost six months into her pregnancy and blooming. She and Jake called round one night with a Christmas present for her, as they wouldn't be around on the actual day, and they were surprised to hear that neither would she.

'Where are you off to, Luce?' her brother asked. 'Skiing?'

She smiled. 'No, not that, although it *is* very cold where I'm going. I'll give you a phone number where you can contact me if you need me.'

Jake eyed her curiously. 'Who are you going with?'

'No one.'

'There's only *you* who would want to be alone at Christmas,' he protested.

'That's right,' she fibbed. 'I need the space. You must remember that I'm with people all the year round. It's good to be alone sometimes.'

'Yes, but at Christmas?' he persisted doubtfully, and she thought that if he didn't let the matter drop she would scream.

'I've got something for you,' she said, changing the subject, and produced a baby's crib, perfume for Melanie and a smart jacket for Jake.

'Thanks, Luce,' he said sincerely when he saw the crib and the other gifts, and when she saw the expression on his face she felt a tight little pain around her heart. Jake wasn't a carefree youth any more. He was a man. The coming child had done that and she was glad. . .glad that he was accepting responsibility at last.

Whatever loose ends there were in her life, she would be going away over Christmas content in the knowledge that he wasn't one of them any more.

Jack Montrose, who had been hovering at a distance ever since the party at the Simmons house, had asked her to go to the Springfield Christmas Ball with him, and in a moment of pique she'd accepted.

He was the last person she wanted to be with, but if Rafe was going to be there with the pouting Justine, she reasoned miserably that *she* might as well turn up with a totally unsuitable partner, too.

It went without saying that Rafe would be there. The ball was the biggest yearly event in the small hospital's fund-raising campaign, and most of the staff from the Infirmary and those from Springfield itself would be there, along with many notable members of the public.

As she dressed for the auspicious occasion the calendar on her wall told her that there were just ten days to Christmas. Ten days to what could have been their first Christmas together. And instead she would be far away in a land that was as cold and frozen as her heart, while Rafe would be secure in the midst of his loving family as they faced their first Christmas without Victoria.

On the face of it it was a sad prospect for him, but she knew that as the miracle of Christmas unfolded all over the world they would be celebrating his mother's life, not her death.

And what would *she* be celebrating? Certainly not being with the man she loved, but at least she would be fulfilling an ambition, going into what was for her unchartered territory in one of the coldest places on earth—and, maybe, just as her job had always filled the gap that the lack of other relationships left, it would do so again. She hoped so.

Apart from the area health authority, Monica, her secretary, and John Adams, her second-in-command, no one knew about her plans. Even Jake had only been given a telephone number, and that was how she wanted it to be.

Not normally a secretive person, Lucinda felt that for

just this once she needed to be separate from the stresses and strains that were present in her life. She needed space to sort out her feelings, to look at the needs that were being denied fulfilment, and time to chart out what looked like being a bleak future. Hopefully she might return at peace with herself and with extra motivation for the job that she loved.

She wore black for the ball. In her present frame of mind the bright colours that enhanced her dark attractiveness seemed inappropriate. She felt as if she was in mourning, and so what could be more suitable than the weeds of it?

It didn't prevent the final effect from being startling, however. She relieved the sombre long-sleeved dress, with its scooped out neckline and flowing panelled skirt, with a long silver chain that swung gently across her breasts as she moved, and the matching bracelet and earrings glittered in the light as brightly as the icicles that hung from the trees outside in the frosty night.

The temperatures had dropped rapidly in the last few days, and when she'd shopped in the town that afternoon there had been fine snow in the air—which was just as well, she thought. It would help to get her acclimatised for the days ahead.

A huge white hat of gleaming fake fur and a heavy beige suede coat with matching lined boots now hung in her wardrobe, and as she'd tried them on in front of her mirror earlier she'd thought wryly that all she needed now was Dr Zhivago by her side. . .or better still Dr Rafe Davidson. . .

Would he realise she was missing over Christmas? she wondered. Would her absence be noted? She'd allowed herself to drift into the realms of fantasy and had bought him a present, telling herself as the assistant in the shop had wrapped a cashmere sweater, that she was playing games, pretending they were on better terms than they were, and that he knew she loved him.

She hadn't any ideas about presenting it to him personally. He would find it on his desk on the last day before she left the country. By doing it that way she wouldn't have to endure his polite thanks, or another distressing dialogue about his intentions with regard to Justine Horrocks.

Jack Montrose had learned his lesson. When he called for her in the early evening he was immaculate in evening dress, impeccably groomed. . .and sober—in every way a most presentable escort. And yet the sight of him didn't make her heart beat any faster.

If she had opened the door to a man with quizzical brown eyes, a pelt of thick russet hair and the most kissable mouth in the world, it would have been different, but she told herself that it was no use yearning for the unattainable, and the smile she dredged up for Jack was warmer than it would have been otherwise.

'Very nice,' he purred when he saw her, and Lucinda gave him a long, level look. If there was one thing she wanted this occasion to have it was dignity. Nothing, but nothing was going to throw her tonight, and so she acknowledged the compliment with a cool nod and led the way to where his car was waiting outside the apartments.

'I was married this time last year,' he said as the car sped along the frost-rimed roads. 'Just goes to show that it doesn't do to rely on anything being permanent in this life, does it?'

She gave him a quick sideways glance. There was enough regret in his voice to show that his new-found freedom wasn't all sweetness and light, and it occurred to her that maybe they'd each chosen the right company for the evening. . .a couple of losers together.

CHAPTER NINE

THEY were all there. Folks she knew, including the curvy Justine, and a lot of them that she didn't. But there was no Rafe. And as the night wore on Lucinda found herself accepting Jack Montrose's attentions with a vague sort of absent-mindedness.

It was strange that he should be missing, she kept telling herself, especially with the Horrocks woman being present, but the fact remained that he was nowhere to be seen. In spite of knowing that he wouldn't have been with her if he *had* been there, Lucinda was choked with disappointment.

Only a matter of days remained now before her leaving the country, and she didn't want to go without one more glimpse of him. All right, they worked in the same building, so he wasn't that much out of reach, but, whereas Rafe was always ready to wander into her department, *she* didn't want to have to go hanging around the cardiac unit to see him. It would be just too humiliating.

Cassandra waved to her from the other side of the dance floor, and, excusing herself from Jack Montrose's company, she went quickly across. Maybe she or Bevan would know why Rafe wasn't there. When she said casually, 'I haven't seen Rafe here tonight. . .' Bevan answered the question that was bugging her.

'You won't have,' he told her. 'He's at the Infirmary. His father had a heart attack earlier in the evening. Rafe went with him in the ambulance and no doubt will be treating him personally.'

'That's awful,' she breathed. 'How serious was the attack?'

'We're not sure,' Cassandra said. 'We thought that we'd leave it for a while and then one of us will ring up to see how he is.'

Lucinda's mind was whirling with dismay. He'd only just lost his mother and now this. 'I'm going to him,' she said, and when Bevan and Cassandra stared at her in surprise she finished lamely, 'I *am* a doctor. There might be something I can do to help.'

'And you're also in love with him, aren't you?' Cassandra said in a low voice, when they were out of Bevan's hearing

She sighed. 'Yes, for what it's worth.'

'I'd say he's a lucky guy, then,' the other woman said reassuringly.

'I don't think that *he* sees it that way,' Lucinda told her, with a level glance at Justine, who at that moment had transferred her attentions to the disconsolate Jack.

'Don't take Rafe's friendship with that one too seriously,' Cassandra said gently. 'He's far too special to get himself hooked up with her.'

'Oh, yes,' she said drily. 'And what would you say, theoretically, of course, if he'd got himself "hooked up" with me?'

Cassandra laughed. 'That he has an eye for quality.'

Lucinda managed a smile. 'You're right about that, he has. And that's why he wouldn't touch me with a barge pole. But I'm wasting time. I'm going to make my apologies to Jack Montrose and then I'll get a taxi to the Infirmary. I only hope that I don't have to ask any favours of management in the near future. After this my name will be mud with the assistant administrator of the trust.'

'I have to leave on an urgent matter, Jack,' she told him when she went back to his side. 'I'm sorry to spoil your evening.'

She was expecting anger, or at least a moan about her leaving him high and dry, but Justine was still hovering and it occurred to her that maybe he'd be glad to see the back of her. After all, she'd been very poor company, and she was thankful that as yet he didn't know why.

As the taxi wove its way through the Saturday-night traffic, Lucinda was trying to work out why Justine Horrocks had been at the ball when Rafe needed the support of his friends, and in particular that of the woman he was seeing such a lot.

If he had been intending to take Justine to the Christmas Ball he would surely have let her know why he couldn't do so, and from there she could have gone to give him what help she could, but there had been no signs of anxiety in her manner and Lucinda could only conclude that either Justine wasn't bothered or she didn't know.

Zoe and young Miles were seated in the waiting room outside the coronary unit when she got to the Infirmary. Rafe's young sister was sobbing quietly and the boy had his arm awkwardly around her shoulders. They looked lost and forlorn and her heart ached for them.

When they saw her framed in the doorway their faces lightened, and Zoe ran across and threw herself into her arms with Miles hovering in the background.

'Isn't it awful, Lucinda?' she sobbed. 'We've lost Mum and now Dad's had a heart attack.'

'Shush,' she comforted softly. 'Rafe's with him, isn't he?'

'Yes.'

'Mmm. Well, he's in good hands, then.' Lucinda looked around her. 'How long have you been here?'

'They brought Dad into Casualty at five o'clock and now he's been transferred up here,' Zoe said wretchedly.

'I'm starving,' Miles told her sheepishly.

'Then go and get some food in the restaurant,' Lucinda told him firmly. 'You'll be no good to anyone if you start collapsing from hunger. . .and you too, Zoe. It will give you something to do.'

'I couldn't eat,' she protested. 'I'd choke.'

'Go and try,' Lucinda coaxed gently, 'and I'll come and find you both if there's any news.'

When they'd gone she went through the swing doors into the coronary unit. The first person she saw was Rafe, deep in conversation with the sister in charge.

She didn't interrupt, just stood quietly behind him waiting for them to finish speaking, but almost as if he sensed her presence he turned slowly and their eyes met.

'Lucinda!' he breathed. 'What's brought *you* here?' He swivelled back to face the nurse. 'Would you excuse me for a moment, Sister?'

'Yes, of course,' Sister murmured. 'I'll be with your father if you want me.'

'I thought you would be at the ball, dancing the night away with that pushy Montrose fellow.'

'I was,' she said quietly, 'until I heard what had happened to your father. How is he, Rafe?'

'Improving, thank God! I was just on my way to reassure Zoe and Miles. Have you seen them?'

'Yes. I've sent them to get something to eat, and promised I'd fetch them immediately if there was any news. What's the situation?'

His face was grave. 'Well, let's say that it was a myocardial infarction and it wasn't a small one. But luckily we got him here quickly and I started to treat him immediately. He's had various medications, such as thrombolytic drugs to prevent clotting, an intravenous infusion of fluids to ward off shock, and electrical defibrillation to counteract arrhythmia.

'Obviously he'll be in Intensive Care for some days and will be carefully monitored, but if all goes to plan he should get over the attack in reasonable time.'

'What about any future problems?'

'Ah, well, that remains to be seen. The ECG shows that there is some damage to the mitral valve, and when I get the results of the blood tests we've taken they could show a similar problem, which might mean surgery in the future.' He raked his hands through the thick copper of his hair. 'But those are tomorrow's problems. Today, my one thought is to keep him alive.

'Dad had been Christmas shopping in the town and was very cold and tired when he got back, apparently. I'd been doing some hoofing around the shops myself and came back to find him slumped in a chair with agonising chest pains ripping at him. I've seen enough heart attacks to know one when I see one, and I had the ambulance out in quick sticks. The rest you know.'

His voice thickened as he went on to say, 'My nightmare was that we were going to lose him as well as Mum in a short space of time, and all the while I was thinking that I was remembering you saying that that was what had happened to you. . .and wishing I'd been more supportive.'

'It was a long time ago,' she said.

'Yes, but it's only a short time since you told *me* about it.'

'I wasn't fishing for sympathy when I told you,' she

said matter-of-factly. 'I was merely trying to explain why my behaviour hasn't always been whiter than white. But we can talk about my past sins another time. . .if you wish. It's your father and the two young ones that you should be concerning yourself about at this moment.'

She supposed he could have taken umbrage at that, but he didn't. He understood what she meant and raised a quizzical eyebrow. 'And you think I'm not? Those two kids have had a rough time of it and so has poor old Dad.'

'And what about you?'

He gave a weary grin. 'I bounce back more quickly. Maybe you've noticed.'

She wondered what that was supposed to mean. In the middle of this in-depth conversation was he telling her that *she* wasn't wreaking havoc in *his* life?

As if determined to confuse her even more, he took her hand and, drawing her towards the doors, said, 'Let's go and find Zoe and Miles and put them out of some of their misery.' Unable to find the strength of will to disentangle herself from his hold, she went with him to where the others were sitting disconsolately in the deserted restaurant.

When they saw Rafe's expression they were both on their feet within a second, and he left Lucinda's side and went to them, holding them close to him as he reassured them.

Lucinda turned away. This wasn't a moment for onlookers, for strangers to be butting in, and while Zoe and Miles smiled their relief she went quietly outside and hailed a taxi.

She usually allowed herself the luxury of a long lie-in on Sunday mornings, but not on this one. The previous night's happenings were too clearly etched in her mind—from the moment that she'd told a disenchanted Jack Montrose that she was leaving him to go to Rafe, to her low-profile exit from the coronary unit.

She would have dearly liked to stay with Rafe, but there'd seemed no point. He knew exactly what he was doing with regard to his father, and he'd had his younger brother and sister there for company. If he'd begged her not to go it would have been different, but he hadn't, and so she'd made her exit, contenting herself with the thought that his father was responding to treatment and that Rafe was coping with his usual easy competence.

Why Justine Horrocks hadn't been there to give him moral support, she didn't know. It must have hurt him to discover that she hadn't thought it necessary, or couldn't be bothered.

Maybe it was going to be his turn to discover that Justine's dainty shoes held clay feet, but then he should already be aware of that. Yet for some reason, he didn't appear to be.

At least *she'd* been there for him. Just as she would be there for him for the rest of his life if he would give her the chance. But apart from anything else, they were too unalike—she with her strong, wilful nature, and he with his humorous, laid-back manner that hid a core of steel. It was an attraction of opposites, all right. Too bad that the yearning for commitment was all on her side.

By seven o'clock she was standing by her lounge window in a bright silk kimono gazing out over the darkened forecourt of the flats and willing daylight to come so that the day could get under way.

Apart from emergencies at the Infirmary or Springfield, she hadn't been up this early on a Sunday in years, and the day was going to seem never-ending, but the fact remained that she couldn't sleep and she'd tossed amongst her fine sheets for long enough.

The itinerary for her forthcoming trip was on the desk in her study and she brought it into the lounge and began to read through it again. It had seemed like a good idea at the time, but now she wasn't so sure that she *did* want to be away over Christmas.

However, the fact remained that she was committed, and there was no way she could drop out at this stage. After all, what made her think that *her* presence over Christmas would make any difference to anybody.

Rafe and his family would cope with this most recent happening as they did with everything else. *He* wasn't pleading for her to be around over Christmas. There'd been no request from him and so she might as well carry on with her own plans as before. At least she wouldn't be surplus to requirements where she was going.

The lights of a car pulling up on the forecourt down below flashed on her ceiling, and when she looked out she saw the two distinctive white stripes on the bonnet. It was Rafe's Mini-Cooper. . .at half past seven on a Sunday morning.

Bliss indeed if he had called to see her at this hour with the urgency of a lover, but there was no likelihood of that with all that he had on his mind at present, and with a certain blonde very much in evidence in his life.

As she went to the door to let him in the soft silk of the kimono brushed against her ankles and clung to her high breasts. The feel of it was gentle as a lover's touch, but it wasn't the touch of silk she craved. It was that of warm, firm flesh on hers, and today of all days the chances of that were nil.

She was dreading seeing sorrow in his face, grief in his

stance, but he looked no different from usual, except tired and unshaven, and she was reminded of that other time, the night of his mother's death, when he'd come to *her* of all people for comfort.

As if reading her thoughts, he smiled briefly. 'You're thinking that I always come to you when I have grief in my life, aren't you?'

The colour crept into Lucinda's smooth cheeks. It was typical of him that the moment he'd crossed her threshold he'd tuned into her thoughts.

'Perhaps,' she said carefully. 'Is that why you're here?'

'No, things are stable at the moment. Dad is resting and Zoe and Miles have gone home to get some sleep. I've left him briefly to call round here to thank you for being there for us last night. It must have ruined your evening.'

She eyed him blankly. What sort of person did he think she was? Some kind of gin-swilling socialite to whom pleasure came first?

There was an overwhelming urge in her to cry out that the evening had been ruined from the moment that she'd seen he wasn't at the ball. . .and that she hadn't been able to get to him quickly enough when she'd heard of the fresh distress that had befallen his family. . .but what was the use?

Rafe seemed determined to keep her on the outer edges of his life, and she supposed it wasn't surprising if he had plans for having a second try with Justine.

The mere fact that he could even contemplate her being bothered about the interrupted evening showed how little he understood her. It seemed that, to him, her stupid behaviour of long ago had branded her forever selfish, and so, with hurt inside her, she said with a brittle smile, 'I noticed that Sir Tom's daughter was conspicuous by her absence at the hospital.'

'I wouldn't have expected Justine to come,' he said. 'She can't stand the thought of anything connected with illness.'

'Tough,' Lucinda said unfeelingly. 'It's to be hoped that she enjoys good health, then, and that you do also when you get back together again.'

If ever there was an opportunity for Rafe to explain his intentions with regard to Justine she'd just provided it, but he didn't take her up on the challenge.

With his dark hazel eyes more serious than she'd ever seen them, he said, as if it were she who was being obtuse, 'Give it a rest, eh, Lucinda. Don't spoil the togetherness we felt last night. Dad is progressing well, considering the severity of the attack. Yesterday evening was a crucial time for all of us and you helped us to get through it. You didn't have to, but you did, and maybe one day we'll be able to do the same for you.'

'We', 'us', he kept saying, not 'I'. Was Rafe deliberately keeping the conversation impersonal? Surely he must see that her presence the night before wasn't just the reflex action of a friend, or someone in health-care.

She was fond of his family, but above all else *he* was the one who mattered. What she'd done had been for him, and if he came up with any more stilted expressions of thanks she would scream.

The itinerary she'd been reading was on the table beside them, with her flight tickets on the top, and Rafe glanced at them casually. Then, his eyes widening, he reached out and picked them up.

'What's this?' he said in a low voice. 'You're flying to *Siberia*, of all places, on the day before Christmas Eve!

Why didn't you tell me? What's going on, Lucinda, and what's all this bumph in the folder?'

'I didn't tell you because I thought you wouldn't be interested,' she told him with an assumed calm. 'The fact that I'm going to Siberia at Christmas time is purely coincidental. It has nothing to do with anything except that some of the best orthopaedic hospitals in the world are situated there, and in the first week of the New Year I'm joining a small group of orthopaedic surgeons who are going to observe techniques.'

His mouth was a straight line, the amber eyes cold as he said, 'Very impressive. I can't think of anyone better fitted to go. But, tell me, why, if the tour of their hospitals isn't until the New Year, are you going before Christmas? When I suggested us spending some time together over the holiday you said you wouldn't be around, and I thought that perhaps you were in the habit of celebrating it with your brother. I never dreamt that you were prepared to spend Christmas with the Mongolians breathing down your neck in the great frozen wastes of Siberia.'

'They *are* civilised out there, you know,' she said, in the same over-calm voice. 'I'm not going to be trudging along behind a pack of huskies, or breaking a hole in the ice to fish for my supper. I'm going early so that I can see something of the country, if you really want to know,' she fibbed.

Her pride wouldn't let her admit that she couldn't bear to spend Christmas on her own again. . .not this time. . . not with him around. . .blowing hot and cold. . .kissing her senseless one minute and having doubts about her the next.

'I see.'

There was a final note in his voice that made her want to throw herself into his arms and tell him that she would stay chained to his side for ever if he would only tell her that he loved her.

'Well, you've made your feelings very clear,' he said, with a sort of bland politeness that hurt far more than harsh words. 'I hope that you enjoy yourself. I've always seen you as a very self-contained person and it obviously isn't going to bother you leaving your friends behind at such a time.'

'Friends!' she cried, with tears threatening. 'Tell me about it!'

'I can see that it's no use talking to you,' he said quietly as he turned to go. 'But then it never is.'

Whenever she saw Rafe during those last few days before Christmas she avoided any sort of conversation. She rang the coronary unit personally each day to ask about his father's progress, and if Rafe thought it uncaring that she hadn't asked *him* about his sick parent it was too bad, as he'd already labelled her that along with other unflattering characteristics.

One afternoon, when she knew that Rafe had gone to see one of his patients who'd been transferred to Springfield, she popped in to see his father and was relieved to find him pottering about and looking quite chirpy.

'Nice to see you, Dr Beckman,' he said when they'd found a couple of vacant chairs in the day room. 'Aren't I the one, eh? Crocking myself up at Christmas.'

Typically, he wasn't having a moan about this happening on top of losing Victoria, and she thought that the pair of them had done an excellent job of raising their family. If ever the unlikely day dawned when she gave birth to a child, the Davidson parents would be her role models.

If her yearnings had borne fruit her children would have

been tiny new shoots from Victoria and Albert's sturdy family tree, but Rafe Davidson had other fish to fry, from what she'd seen, and she thought with grim amusement that she was too long in the tooth to wait for Miles to grow up.

'What are you doing for Christmas, my dear?' Rafe's father asked with a glance at her sombre face.

Lucinda managed a smile. 'I'm going to Siberia, of all places. I'm having a few days' holiday in Moscow first, and then spending a period of observation in some hospitals out there.'

'Really? That sounds fascinating. What did Rafe have to say?'

'Quite a lot.'

'Er. . .I see. But he *is* very pressured at the moment, you know. Keeping an eagle eye on me and watching over the young ones—not to mention this fixation he seems to have for Justine, Tom Simmons's daughter. I don't suppose he ever expected her to turn up husbandless, but that's how it appears to be. What she's done with the fellow, I don't know, but from what I've seen he isn't around.'

'I don't think Victoria would have been too happy about him seeing her so often,' he said with a frown, 'as she hurt him badly once, and he's been wary of getting too involved with the opposite sex ever since. I'm not all that keen on the arrangement myself, but Tom and his wife seem all for it.'

I'm not exactly tickled to death with it either, Lucinda thought dismally, especially as you've just confirmed what I've been thinking all along. How dared Rafe tell me there was nothing between them when everyone knows about it?

'I will be in here for Christmas, I'm afraid,' Albert Davidson was saying. 'It's a disappointment, in one way, but at least Rafe and the young ones won't have the worry of looking after me during the holiday.'

'I suppose they'll spend most of the time here with you,' she said, striving to keep the envy out of her voice.

He smiled. 'It's very likely, but I don't want them tied to me all over Christmas. They have their own lives to lead, like yourself.'

When she got up to go Lucinda said softly, 'No need to mention my visit to Rafe.'

He looked at her with kindly blue eyes and said, 'Are you saying that the two of you are not communicating?'

'You could say that, and I don't want him to think that I'm pushing myself as far as his family are concerned.'

'He's not likely to think that,' he protested mildly.

Don't bet on it, she thought bleakly, but as she went back to her own part of the hospital the memory of the brief harmonious time she'd spent with Albert Davidson took the chill from her heart.

'You've had a call from Springfield while you were away,' Monica informed her when she went back to the office.

'What about?' she asked listlessly. It was late afternoon and she'd been hoping for an early finish to start getting herself organised for the forthcoming trip.

That was one reason why she was less than enthusiastic about the message, and another was that Rafe had gone to the Community Hospital and she didn't want to come across him if they wanted her over there for some reason.

'Ethan Lassiter says that there has been an accident at the forestry centre on the Cirencester route and they've taken the victim into Springfield because it was nearest.'

'What sort of injuries?' she asked, with her flagging interest reviving.

'Multiple fractures.'

Lucinda frowned. 'I'd rather they'd brought him here if tricky surgery is going to be called for.'

'Apparently the guy went into shock in the ambulance and his heart stopped beating,' her secretary explained. 'Ethan knew you would prefer to have him here, but he said that he's not fit to move and so will you go there?'

She was already putting on her heavy top coat and grabbing her bag. 'Ask John to take my clinic, will you, if I'm not back in time?'

Monica eyed her doubtfully. 'He was hoping to go Christmas shopping.'

Lucinda glared at her. 'Tough! So was I.'

When she went into the small casualty area at Springfield the first person she saw was Rafe, bending over an inert figure in a cubicle opposite the door.

At the draught of cold air that she brought in with her he turned and, as if they'd never had the tight-lipped altercation in her flat early on Sunday morning, said, 'Hello, Lucinda. I thought *you* might be bringing up the rear. I was here when they brought this fellow in and took over with the cardiac problem. Did they tell you that his heart stopped in the ambulance? Only for a matter of seconds, fortunately, but it was touch and go.'

She nodded without speaking. He was acting as if they were on good terms. Not lover-like, but friendly, and she thought that even their disagreements had so little impact on him that he forgot them as quickly as he did their more passionate moments.

'We've already had him in X-ray, Dr Beckman,' Isobel Graham said as Lucinda put on a white coat. 'Here are the plates.'

Lucinda groaned when she saw them. 'Are there any bones that aren't broken? Whatever happened to him?'

'The forestry commission were felling trees and he didn't move fast enough when they yelled "timber",' Rafe informed her. 'It's amazing he wasn't killed. I've known a few fatalities from falling trees.'

'Yes, well, we'll have him in Theatre as quickly as possible, Sister,' she said stiffly, determined that even if he was all chummy again, she wasn't going to be the same.

As a porter began to wheel the stretcher trolley out of Casualty, with Isobel Graham supervising, Rafe said with a casualness that set her teeth on edge, 'I'll come into Theatre with you. The heart seems to be stable now, but after a shock of that kind there could still be a chance of some degree of ventricular fibrillation. But before we get bogged down in there, tell me, are you still intending spending Christmas with the abominable snowmen?'

'Yes,' she said decisively. 'And who knows? I might be so impressed with their orthopaedic practices out there that I decide to stay.'

The forestry worker was indeed badly injured. The paramedics who had attended him at the scene and in the ambulance had suspected spinal damage, and he had been carefully handled accordingly while desperate attempts to achieve a return of the heartbeat had been taking place.

The X-rays showed fractures of the ribs, tibia of the left leg, the collarbone on the same side of the body, and the left wrist. Also, more seriously, there was an unstable fracture of the spine.

Mike Drew, the GP in attendance, had just arrived and he came hurrying to join them after hearing what had happened.

'I'm not happy about this, Mike,' Lucinda said tetchily as she scrubbed up in Springfield's small theatre. 'This man's injuries are so severe he should have been taken directly to the Infirmary. There are deep lacerations as well as the fractures, and did you know that he suffered cardiac failure on the way here?'

The likeable GP's face was grave. 'I get your point Lucinda. It's hardly fair to expect you to do this sort of surgery here at Springfield, but if anybody can cope... you can, and Rafe and I are here to assist. At least the poor guy has got the brains of the cardiac unit on hand if there are any further problems with the heartbeat, along with—'

'Beckman the Bone Woman?' Rafe finished for him.

Mike smiled. 'I've heard you called some things. . .'

'And none of them complimentary,' she commented drily.

For the next four hours they worked as a team in every sense of the word, with Mike as anaesthetist and Rafe and herself dealing with the spinal dislocation, where she manipulated the affected bones back into place while the patient was under a general anaesthetic.

Then the ribs were strapped up, and the arm with the fractured collarbone put in a sling, and finally she performed an external fixation of the broken tibia, by inserting metal pins that slotted into a frame through the skin and into the bone.

When they had finished, and the injured man was about to be taken to the recovery room, Lucinda passed a weary hand across her brow and with the other indicated the frame. 'That is what my visit to Siberia is connected with,' she said, still with an edge to her voice. 'We in this country have been treating fractures and deformities of the bone in that way for some time, but a Russian called Gavril Ilizarov was doing that kind of surgery years before we even thought of it.'

'Knowing what the authorities were like in those sorts of countries, they kept the knowledge to themselves for a long time, and it is only recently that we in the West have been allowed access to their superlative orthopaedic institutes.'

'Ilizarov first used the technique on wounded soldiers many years ago and found that fractures and bone non-alignments healed more quickly and more successfully, in many cases, than after being encased in plaster.'

'His simple technique of holding the bone in position with spikes and the frame was responsible for a break-through in orthopaedic surgery.'

Both men had listened to her attentively, and when she'd finished speaking, Mike said, 'It sounds fascinating, Lucinda. When exactly are you going?'

'In a couple of day's time,' she told him, averting her eyes from Rafe's reproachful gaze.

'You're going to be there over Christmas!' Mike exclaimed. 'Well, I shouldn't think there'll be any shortage of snow, but surely the sightseeing round the hospitals and the lectures won't be taking place over the holiday?'

'Er. . .no,' she replied stiffly. 'I'm going early to do some sightseeing of my own, not connected with the NHS.'

When Mike had gone on his rounds of Springfield's small complex Rafe said evenly, 'I wonder if Mike would go gallivanting off to some God-forsaken place just to get away from his friends and relations.'

That stung her into anger. 'My relation. . .and you will note that I speak in the singular. . .has never craved my company at Christmas since he reached his teens. Jake is going to stay with his girlfriend's parents and won't be back until after the New Year.'

'As to my friends, the few that I have accumulated over past years are usually fully booked with family commitments at this time of the year, as you are yourself. So they aren't going to miss me either. And if you're including yourself in that same category I can't see *you* missing me, not with sweet Justine to hold your hand.'

'You're crazy!' he snapped angrily. 'There is a very good reason why I'm spending so much time with her and it has nothing to do with us. . .'

She didn't let him finish. 'I'll bet it doesn't! With my reputation I don't qualify as anything more than an aperitif. Your petite blonde friend is the main course!'

They were facing each other like stormy adversaries and she thought miserably that she'd got to him at last, made him lose his temper. But there wasn't a grain of satisfaction in it.

'I have to go,' she told him tonelessly as weariness overcame her annoyance and hurt. 'I have much to do during the next forty-eight hours.'

'Don't let *me* hold you back,' he retaliated. 'But then you wouldn't, would you?'

CHAPTER TEN

WHEN she left Springfield Lucinda headed for home. The day staff on the orthopaedic unit at the Infirmary would be long gone, and if there had been anything for her to go back for Monica would have contacted her at the Community Hospital.

She'd thought that Rafe might leave at the same time, but he'd been chatting to Ethan Lassiter when she'd gathered up her belongings and made a determined exit. Yet by the time she pulled up at traffic lights a couple of miles along the road she saw that the racing green Mini was behind her in the queue of cars, waiting for the lights to change.

He would have no choice but to go back to the Infirmary, she thought. There would be his father to check on—the elderly heart attack victim would be anxious for a glimpse of his son.

She was feeling less fraught now. Her irritation of earlier in the afternoon had gone, and she told herself that maybe it was because she'd enjoyed working with the two very competent doctors.

They'd been a hurriedly assembled team, but it hadn't impeded their speed and efficiency, and when the injured man regained consciousness he would find—painfully, no doubt, but reassuringly so—that his injuries had been dealt with.

She was ravenous and would have liked to stop off at a restaurant. Not the Wang Su, this time, but somewhere classy and relaxing. But she decided that time was of the essence and it would have to be a tin of soup back at the flat.

When she'd finished sorting out what clothes she was going to take with her on the trip, and had realised ruefully that warm winter clothes took up a lot more space than summer flimsies, Lucinda gift-wrapped the sweater that she'd bought for Rafe.

Once that was accomplished she wrote in her bold, flamboyant hand on the card attached to it. *'I may "run out" on my friends at Christmas, but I don't forget them. Love Lucinda.'*

Their relationship was going nowhere, she thought miserably. They were so different in temperament it just wasn't true. Added to that, she felt that he still disapproved of her, and then there was Justine Horrocks. . .

The list of reasons for making herself scarce over the holidays was never-ending, but she couldn't let Christmas pass without a gift for the man she loved, and tomorrow, last thing before she left the Infirmary for the next two and a half weeks, she would leave it on his desk.

Hopefully her last day would pass without further sightings of him and then she would be free to pursue her plans. She'd never felt less enthusiastic about anything in her life.

The Siberian visit was different. That was connected with the job. She'd long wanted to view the orthopaedic practices in that part of the world and she'd no regrets about going there. It was the fact that she'd let herself in for mooning around Moscow for over a week on her own before travelling to the Siberian Institute that she was having second thoughts about.

Until recently her career had been the all-consuming interest in her life, until a certain copper-haired man had shown her that existence wasn't all bed and work. That because she wasn't the world's biggest success when it came to personal relationships it didn't mean that she would never find the right man.

She'd found him, but her rejoicings had been brief, and to this day she still didn't understand why she was being so defeatist about him. Why wasn't she fighting tooth and nail?

Was it pride? Because she'd never been much good at showing humility? Whatever it was, she couldn't squabble over Rafe with his honey-blonde ex-fiancée, and, if *she* was too proud, what was *he*? A weakling for going meekly back to someone who'd left him once?

But he wasn't a weakling, was he? He could be as tough as herself if the occasion demanded it, and, for some reason that only he knew, he was prepared to make allowances for Justine when he'd been only too quick to criticise herself.

Stop fretting over the man! she told herself as she showered before getting into bed. Act your age!

But she *was* acting her age, that was the trouble, and as she dried herself in the bathroom of what Rafe had described as her space-age flat she paused, absently eyeing her coltish nakedness in the mirror.

How would it feel if Rafe were reflected in the mirror beside her, with dark gold body hair, strong flanks, a hard chest, and the rest of his male parts fashioned for her delight? A sigh escaped her. Don't cry for the moon, she told herself. There will be others. But she didn't really believe that.

Her last day was hectic, and when lunchtime came Lucinda dashed into the town to get herself a new watch-strap as the existing one had snapped that morning while she was dressing.

In a large jeweller's on the main street she was dismayed to find Justine Horrocks in front of her at the counter, and just as Lucinda was about to turn on her heel and go elsewhere the other woman swung round and saw her.

'Hello, there,' she said casually, with a smug little smile, and turned back to where the assistant was putting a small velvet box into an expensive mini-carrier bag.

'I hope that you will both be happy with the way we have done the alteration,' the girl behind the counter said. 'We have replaced the original stone with a more expensive one, as Dr Davidson specially requested.'

Dread was gripping Lucinda. Rafe had bought Justine a ring! It could only mean one thing. She'd lost him. She had stood by like a wet lettuce and let another woman ensnare him. As if tuning into her thoughts, Justine let her tinkling laugh ring out.

'If you remember, he did say that only the very best was good enough,' she reminded the girl, and then added eyeing Lucinda from under half-closed lids, 'What more can a woman ask than that?'

Lucinda turned away. The last picture she wanted in her mind as she left the country was that of Rafe putting a beautiful ring on Justine's small claw, and with a haste that scattered those who'd followed her into the shop she steamed out.

There was no dithering about her now. She *was* doing the right thing. Leaving the Midlands town where she'd put down indifferent roots and spending a solitary Christmas in a far land.

The only thing that remained to be done was to place Rafe's gift in his office and hope that he wouldn't see anything strange in the gesture.

The sweater seemed a mediocre thing compared to his

purchase for Justine, but she reckoned it was suitable for an acquaintance to give him, and that was all she was.

Also, if she were to give him a more personal thing and it brought forth polite surprise, it would leave her squirming. Yet hadn't she been doing that for weeks without success? Offering him the most personal gifts of all: her heart, her mind and her willing body?

At just gone six o'clock she heard him start the bike outside her office window, and within seconds it had zoomed off, leaving the coast clear. She quickly made her way to his part of the building.

For once the tinsel-decked corridor was empty. The huge, efficient machine that was the Infirmary was getting ready to settle down for the night, and behind the closed doors of its wards the sick were preparing to face Christmas in its confines.

As she'd expected, Rafe's office was empty, and she put the gift carefully in the centre of his desk. There was guilt inside her because this was to be her only contribution to his Christmas, and his angry taunt about her running away rang in her ears.

Did the Davidsons need her? she questioned uneasily. *Were* they going to be lost and forlorn with Victoria gone and Albert a heart attack victim?

She straightened her shoulders. Hardly, if the small velvet box she'd seen Justine collect from the jeweller's earlier in the day was anything to go by. It would be a time for celebrations all round from the looks of it.

As she turned to leave Lucinda heard a sound from the next office, and as she listened it came again, a sort of sobbing groan.

She knocked on the door gently, and when there was no

answer pushed it back to reveal a huddled figure seated at the desk.

'Sir Thomas!' she said in surprise. 'Are you all right?' It was the inevitable question that one asked at the sight of another's distress, she thought, and the most stupid.

It was clear that the elderly consultant was *not* all right, if his ravaged countenance was anything to go by, and immediately she guessed that this was something to do with his general deterioration over the past few weeks.

'Are you ill?' she asked, using a more sensible approach.

He shook his head and got to his feet. 'No, Dr Beckman. Just weary of mind.' As if to let her see that that was all he had to say on the subject he said with an attempt at his usual heavy joviality, 'Rafe tells me that you're off to Siberia tomorrow?'

'Er. . .yes. . .' she replied, taken aback that the conversation had suddenly switched to her affairs.

'What time are you flying out?'

'I'm on a flight to Moscow in the early evening from Heathrow. I'm spending Christmas and New Year there, and then travelling on to Siberia for ten days.'

'We'll be in the airport ourselves about that time,' he said heavily, and Lucinda eyed him in surprise.

'You're going away for Christmas, too?'

'No. I'm afraid not. We're merely seeing someone off.'

'Oh, I see.'

She was only mildly interested. At this second the Simmons family weren't exactly her favourite people, especially as Sir Tom and his wife seemed to look upon Rafe's attachment to their daughter so favourably. But it didn't mean that she wasn't concerned for the older man's health, and she offered, 'Can I run you home?'

He shook his head. 'I've got the car here.'

'Yes, I know, but I thought that as you don't seem yourself. . .'

He sighed. 'I'm not. That's true enough. But I can manage, thanks.'

Driving home, Lucinda went over the strange conversation in her mind. Something was certainly bugging Sir Tom, but he obviously wanted to keep it to himself and she didn't blame him for that.

Hurts of the mind and heart didn't always improve when brought out into the open. Often the attitude of others towards them made them worse, as she'd discovered to her cost, but the change in the man was incredible, and if he went on like this his health *would* be affected.

Zoe came on the phone just after she'd got back to the flat, and when she heard her voice Lucinda felt her heart skip a beat. Her first thought was for Albert, but all was well in that direction, and it appeared that she hadn't rung about anything to do with Rafe. His young sister wanted to know if she had a recipe for a Christmas cake, and when she heard the request Lucinda began to laugh.

'You're asking the wrong person, I'm afraid,' she told her. 'I can tell you all the ingredients for a new knee joint, and what to do with them, but with regards to a Christmas cake! Aren't the shops still open?'

Zoe gurgled at the other end of the phone. 'Good idea. I'll whizz round there now. . .and Lucinda. . .?'

'Ye-es?' she asked warily.

'Are you *really* going to be away all over Christmas?'

She closed her eyes. It was incredible. In past years no one had ever given a damn what she did with herself over the festive period, but this time, because she'd reluctantly decided to make herself scarce, everybody wanted her around—although in Rafe's case she suspected it was for selfish reasons, such as having an older woman around for the rest of his family. But the plaintive note in Zoe's voice made her want to cry. 'No. It's not true. I'll be here!'

But did she want that? To be the eternal gooseberry again while Rafe and his odious blonde flashed around the place together? No way. So she told Zoe regretfully, 'I'm afraid so. 'But perhaps when I get back we can see something of each other?'

'I'd like that,' the girl said shyly. 'I miss Mum such a lot.'

Lucinda's throat closed up. Poor kid! The fact that she saw her as more of a mother substitute than a contemporary didn't bother her. After all, she supposed she *was* old enough to be Zoe's mother. . .if she'd been a reasonably youthful bride.

When the young girl had gone off the phone she stood looking out onto the winter's night. If anything else happened to make her doubt the wisdom of what she was doing she could see herself unpacking and preparing to face the holiday in her usual solitary state, but at home.

The second time the phone rang it was Jake, and at the sound of his voice her heart rejoiced again. There was a new maturity in his manner, even though his greeting was typical of the old Jake.

'Hi, Luce. How's things?' he wanted to know, and she found herself smiling wryly at the question. What would he say if she told him, Deadly?

'Fine, thanks,' she told him, wishing fervently that they were.

'You all ready for off?' he asked.

'Mmm. Sort of.'

'I wish you weren't going,' he said suddenly, and she

goggled at the receiver. Whenever had Jake ever craved her presence? What was going on? It seemed as if the fates were ganging up on her. All it needed now was for a message to come through to say that the Siberian trip had been cancelled. If that happened then her long trek to Moscow would be pointless.

But maybe Jake had a very good reason for wanting her near, and she asked anxiously, 'Why? Is Melly not well?'

'No, she's fine. It's just that I don't like the thought of you spending Christmas on your own,' he said awkwardly.

It was on the tip of her tongue to tell him that it had never bothered him before but she bit the words back. Why spoil the new relationship that was forming between them?

'That's very sweet of you,' she said with a wobble in her voice, 'but don't worry about me. Just look after Melly and yourself. That's all I ask of you.'

It was his turn to sound choked as he said, to her amazement, 'I love you, Luce,'

'And I love you, too,' she said huskily.

For the rest of the evening Lucinda was plagued with a feeling of unreality. She'd had Zoe and Jake wanting her to stay at home over Christmas—two requests that she'd never have expected—and it made her feel warm inside.

But the plea that she really wanted to hear must come from the man she loved, and apart from the occasion when he'd made it clear that *he* didn't want her to go either, but had then soured the moment by not being prepared to give her any good reasons why, he hadn't mentioned it again.

And, realising after the episode in the jeweller's that he was prepared to be second best to the woman who had him running the moment she crooked her greedy finger, she didn't think it was likely to be forthcoming.

She was wrestling with a silk blouse that was an absolute

pain to iron when she heard the screech of a motorcycle pulling up outside. The drapes were shut but through a crack at the side she could see the forecourt of the flats. Her spirits plummeted as its rider reversed and sped off into the night on a machine that was nothing like Rafe's.

It was ironic. She was in everyone's thoughts except his. For some reason her mind went back to the day they'd met, at Imogen's christening. Cassandra had given her the baby to hold and she'd been irritated that the noise of his bike had startled Imogen.

There'd been a strange feeling inside her as the laughing hazel eyes had looked into hers. . .a feeling that something special was about to happen. . .and it had. She'd fallen in love with a quixotic man, and yet if he were to walk into the room at this instant what was left of her resolve to stay away from him would disappear like Siberian snow on a brazier.

She was intending leaving at midday, which would give her time to drive to London and allow the regulation couple of hours requested by the airways before take-off.

As the morning progressed she found herself willing the phone to ring, willing Rafe to add his pleas to those of Zoe and Jake. Yet she knew that if he did come on the line it wouldn't be for that. It would be to thank her for the sweater, or some other matter of minor importance. But the telephone stayed silent until a quarter of an hour before she was due to leave.

Flinging herself across the room to answer it, Lucinda felt her mind racing. What would she say to him? That she'd seen Justine at the jewellery counter and were congratulations in order?

Though did she want to deliberately inflict pain upon

herself? Maybe, as it was better to know the worst than keep hoping she might be wrong.

It wasn't Rafe's voice that spoke in her ear when she lifted the receiver and she went limp with disappointment. It was a woman's and for a moment she didn't recognise it.

'Dr Beckman?'

'Er. . .yes?'

'Nora Simmons speaking. I'm ringing to ask a favour of you.'

Lucinda stared at the receiver as if the lady in question were concealed in its plastic mouthpiece. Whatever could Sir Tom's wife want with her today of all days? She hardly knew the woman.

'What is it that you want of me, Lady Simmons?' she asked, trying to conceal her amazement. 'Only I have to point out that I'm due to leave for Heathrow in a matter of minutes.'

'That is why I'm ringing you,' the other woman said agitatedly. 'We are going there ourselves and I wondered if I could ask you for a lift, as Thomas has just decided that he isn't fit to be in charge of the car this morning, and I don't drive.'

Lucinda stifled a groan. The last thing she wanted was to be in contact with any of the Simmons family, but obviously the elderly consultant hadn't forgotten their conversation of the previous day and it would be ungracious not to agree to his wife's request,

'Yes, of course I'll take you,' she said quickly, hoping that her reluctance wasn't obvious. 'The only thing is that I need to get off almost immediately.'

She could almost hear Nora Simmons' sigh of relief. 'That's fine by us,' she said. 'We'll be ready and waiting.'

'Us', she'd said, Lucinda thought as she stacked her

luggage in the boot of the Mercedes. So although he wasn't fit to drive Tom Simmons must be intending accompanying her. But when she got to the house he opened the door to her in his dressing gown, looking even more haggard than the previous day.

'Thank you, my dear,' he said shakily as she picked up the case that was standing in the gracious hallway. 'Both Nora and I are deeply obliged to you.'

Lucinda patted his arm comfortingly, ashamed of her original reluctance to help out. 'Don't worry about a thing,' she told him reassuringly. 'I'll get your wife safely to Heathrow, but I'm concerned about how she's going to get back if she is merely seeing someone off.'

His face reddened. 'She'll come back by train, of course.' As he heard footsteps on the stairs, he added, 'Here they are now.'

Lucinda's jaw dropped. 'They', he'd said, and 'they' it was. His heavy-bosomed wife, looking almost as ravaged as he, was accompanied by her daughter. The fact that they were both warmly wrapped against the cold in expensive top coats was enough to make Lucinda realise that Justine wasn't on her way to the corner shop.

Her parents gave no explanation of Justine's presence and neither did she. Without a word of greeting she settled herself in the back seat of the car and gazed stonily through the window as it pulled away from the house.

If no one was going to tell her why Justine was included in the party, she was damned if she was going to ask, Lucinda decided, and it was left to Lady Simmons to keep the conversation going as they sped along the motorways to London.

Maybe Justine was going to meet the missing husband, Lucinda thought with a sudden lift of spirits. But Tom had said they were seeing someone off, not meeting them, so it couldn't be that. And whose was the case that she'd placed next to her own in the boot? It became more curious by the minute.

When they got to the terminal building Lucinda pulled up at the entrance and the Simmonses, mother and daughter, got out of the car and waited while she got the case out.

Justine looked down on it with blank blue eyes and Lucinda was tempted to say, 'Don't think that I'm going to carry it, my lovely. I have my own stuff to see to, and even if I hadn't I don't owe you any favours.'

There was something wrong here, but she didn't know what. For instance, where was Rafe, the attentive suitor? And who were the over-talkative mother and morose daughter about to see off?

Whatever the answer, she hadn't time to be concerning herself over their affairs. She'd done as she was asked and now she intended to bid them a brisk farewell.

As if guessing her thoughts, Nora Simmons said gratefully, 'Thanks, Dr Beckman. We can manage fine from here.'

Lucinda nodded. 'That's good, Lady Simmons, as I have to park my car and check in my baggage before I can relax.' She glanced briefly at the woman who had spoilt her chances with Rafe. 'Bye for now,' she said, and, getting back into the car, she drove off.

With the preliminaries over, she settled down with a coffee and a magazine to await her flight call. The monitors indicated that it was on time, and in an hour and a half she expected to hear the call to board.

There were just twenty minutes to go when a hand on her shoulder had her twisting round in her seat, and when she looked up Nora Simmons was gazing down on her.

Her face was tear-stained and blotchy, and when Lucinda got quickly to her feet and asked what was wrong the older woman sank down onto the seat Lucinda had just vacated and said chokingly, 'She's gone!'

'Who's gone?'

'Justine, of course,' Lady Simmons said wearily. 'Gone back to Canada to face the music. Her flight just took off.'

Lucinda felt as if her legs would give way as she tried to grapple with what Nora Simmons had just said. The selfish little blonde had deserted Rafe again. . . That was her first thought, and the second was, What music was her mother referring to?

'I'm afraid I don't understand,' she said stiffly. 'You're saying that your daughter has gone back to Canada? It was *her* that you were seeing off?'

'Yes, of course. Who did you think it was?'

'From what your husband said to me yesterday I understood you were travelling to Heathrow to see *someone* off, and I took it to be friends that he was referring to. Even when Justine got in the car this morning it never occurred to me that he was alluding to her. I was under the impression that she was going with you for company because Sir Thomas wasn't well.'

'If that were all. . .' her mother said sadly. 'When she arrived unexpectedly all those weeks ago we were thrilled. She told us that Logan couldn't come with her because he was too busy at the office, and as we've never really taken to him it was a bonus. What we didn't know was that he's on bail, awaiting trial for embezzlement, and that Justine is implicated, too. She'd ran off and left him to face the music.

'The only person she's been able to talk to is Rafe. She battened on to him like a limpet the moment she arrived and confided in him, with the result that he has spent weeks trying to persuade her to go back and support her husband by facing up to what she's done.

'Tom and I only found out what was going on recently and it has nearly killed him. He's a proud man, and the thought of having a daughter who is no better than a common criminal was unbearable.

'With regard to Rafe, Justine, in her conceit, thought she could weave her old spell over him, but she was sadly mistaken. How he has put up with her pestering and whingeing, I'll never know.

'Thomas and I were only too pleased to see them together again before we found out what she'd been up to. We have a great regard for him, and Justine had told us that her marriage was over. But once she realised that Rafe was out of her reach for ever, Justine gave up trying to take up where they'd left off and reluctantly decided to go back to Vancouver. On the promise that her father and I will be out there just as soon as Tom is well enough, she boarded the flight that's just left.'

'And where is Rafe today?' Lucinda asked through dry lips.

'With his father, I presume. I think he would have made the effort to come with us if she'd asked him, as he's a kind and generous man, but my daughter lost interest the moment she accepted that he hadn't the slightest affection for her in the romantic sense.

'It's been a hard lesson for her to learn, and there is an even harder one awaiting her when she gets back to Canada.' She wiped her eyes and her voice was less fraught as she said, 'Justine was always a greedy little girl, wanting what belonged to her friends, and that greed made her take money that wasn't hers. Now she must accept the consequences.

'As for her father and I, we will be everlastingly grateful to Rafe for having the patience and kindness to make her see that there was only one thing to be done. She has monopolised his free time for weeks, but at last it's over, and I'm sure that he's just as relieved as we are.'

Lucinda was reeling at the revelations unfolding before her. It would take time for joy to take the place of misery. In the meantime her flight was due to be announced any moment, and in front of her was a distressed elderly woman that she just couldn't abandon.

'I'm going to get you a cup of tea before anything else,' she said tightly, 'and then I'll get you a taxi to take you to the station.' She looked anxiously at the grieving mother. 'And promise me that you will go straight home to your husband.'

'Yes, of course,' Lady Simmons said wearily. 'Where else would I go'

By the time Lucinda had sorted out Nora Simmons, a voice was asking over the loud speaker system if passenger Beckman would please make her way to the departure gate for the flight to Moscow.

And because what she had been told was only just sinking in, and it didn't alter the fact that even though Rafe had no commitment to Justine Horrocks there was nothing to say that he was in love with herself, she hurried on board and slumped down into her seat.

Closing her eyes, she tried to sort out her thoughts, but even now there was to be no peace. 'Dr Beckman?' a polite voice said at her elbow, and when she opened them a young stewardess was holding out a huge bouquet.

'For me?' she gasped, by now feeling that there was nothing left to surprise her. But she was wrong. '*I love you, Lucinda,*' Rafe had written on the card. '*Come home.*

There's nobody to fill my stocking!'

'Excuse me,' she cried as she hurried down the gangway. 'Please don't close the doors, I want to get off. Rafe loves me!'

A man seated nearby tutted grumpily and said, 'Typical woman! keeps us all waiting and then wants to get off!' But others eyed her with amusement, and the cabin crew, who'd read the message on the card and had been placing bets as to her reaction, bowed her out onto the steps that led to the tarmac and waved her towards an empty buggy that had just deposited the last lot of luggage.

She watched the plane take off from a distance and had no regrets. The plea she'd longed for had come on the heels of Nora Simmons's revelations and she couldn't wait to do as he asked.

Her eyes were huge dark pools of happiness as, still clutching the flowers, she got behind the wheel of her car that had no sooner been parked than it was back on the road.

The miles seemed to crawl by as Lucinda drove back to the town that she'd left a few hours earlier, but she could bear it because at the end of her journey there was Rafe.

She couldn't make up her mind whether to go to the flat first to freshen up, or straight to the Davidson house. But something told her that in the day's last hours Rafe would be with his father.

They were two men preparing to face a Christmas without the women they loved. In Rafe's case it was twofold, as not only had he lost his mother but he would now be visualising herself high in the clouds, heading for the Soviet capital.

However, he was in for a surprise. At this moment he wouldn't know whether his flowers and the poignant note with them had reached her before take-off, but he soon would. Her body warmed at the thought that within minutes she would be in his arms, with all the doubts and dismay behind her and the way ahead clear for once in her life.

CHAPTER ELEVEN

THE great stone bulk of the Infirmary lay sleeping as Lucinda drove into the sparsely occupied car park, and as her eyes raked its shadows she caught the bright gleam of metal.

It was the BMW. She'd guessed right. He was here. And now that the moment she'd been living for had arrived her palms were moist and her throat dry.

What was she going to say to him? Dash in and blurt out that she loved him, too? She smiled. What did it matter? They would have the rest of their lives to say all the things that were in their hearts.

The small side-ward on the coronary unit was dimly lit, and when she opened the door she could barely make out the figure in the bed, let alone the man slumped in a chair beside it, but after the first few seconds her eyes became accustomed to the gloom and she saw that they were both fast asleep. The patient was lying comfortably on pristine sheets and his visitor was slumbering awkwardly, with his head propped on his hand.

Rafe's hair was tousled, his chin bristly, and his new sweater was crumpled. She looked down on him tenderly. He'd worn her gift on the first day of receiving it, and while all the world was getting ready to enjoy itself this man was keeping a vigil over his sick father. Then he would be going home to a house from which the focal point had gone, and the two youngsters there needed him almost as much as she did.

He stirred in his sleep and she touched his face with gentle fingers. He made to brush them away, as if thinking it was an insect, and in so doing his hand touched hers and became still.

As he opened his eyes their hazel depths observed her in startled disbelief, and then he was on his feet. 'Lucinda!' he muttered quietly as he took both of her hands in his. 'I can't believe what I'm seeing! What made you change your mind?'

Her smile lit up the dark room. 'Well, for starters I had a heart-to-heart with Lady Simmons in the airport lounge, and she put me wise about a few things.'

'You met Nora Simmons at Heathrow?' he said in further amazement. 'How come?'

'Not only did I meet her, I took them there...to the airport... Nora and her uncommunicative daughter—totally unaware that the woman I'd mistakenly thought to be my rival for your affections was going back to where she'd come from. I must be stupid but it never dawned on me. Sir Tom had spun me the yarn that they were going to the airport to see someone off.'

'But they were,' he said in the same stunned tones. 'Justine.'

She laughed softly, and there was a world of joy in it. 'Yes, I know that now, but I didn't when I got myself lumbered with them. And lo and behold, while I was killing time until my Moscow flight, the fly in the ointment was soaring above me on her way back to Canada.'

'Did Lady S tell you what had been going on?' he asked, with his eyes devouring her face and his hands tightening their grip.

Lucinda's face sobered. 'Yes, she did, and why in the

name of heaven you didn't put me in the picture I'll never know.'

His expression was as sober as her own. 'Justine made me promise that I wouldn't tell anyone the reason why she'd left Canada in such a hurry, not even her parents. They only found out recently when I insisted that she tell them, and you've seen what it's done to Tom.

'If you remember, I've kept trying to convince you that there was nothing between us, but it was difficult to make it sound believable because of my promise to her.'

'I won't argue with that,' she told him wryly. 'Perhaps you can explain what it was that she was collecting from the jeweller's yesterday on your behalf? It was in a small velvet box and she was positively cooing over it. From her attitude and the comments of the shop assistant I was convinced that it was a ring.'

His smile was rueful. 'It sounds as if Justine was putting on a show for your benefit. It was a pendant, a Christmas gift for Zoe that she'd offered to collect for me. The chain was just what that young sister of mine will approve of, but the stone wasn't to my liking and I'd asked the shop to change it for a better quality one.'

Her radiance was dimmed for a second. 'I was so miserable I couldn't get out of there quickly enough,' she told him.

'Well, there you have it,' he said with a smile. 'It wasn't a ring, as you thought. There is only one woman I am prepared to buy a ring for and at that moment she wasn't having anything to do with me. After my stupid comment when you told me about your youthful escapade with Bevan's brother nothing I did was right.'

She laughed and her eyes adored him. 'Oh, I don't know. I can remember the odd occasion when what you did was so right I was wilting with longing for days afterwards. But it's true that I was peeved at what you said when I told you about Darren. I'd had years of the cold shoulder from Bevan and then his bosom buddy appeared on the scene and joined in the act! How did you expect me to feel?'

'Did you know why I said it?' he asked, as his voice deepened.

'I had a pretty good idea. I thought it was because you were so perfect yourself—that you had such high standards that you couldn't tolerate anyone like me.'

'Rubbish,' he snorted. 'It was because I'd just found the woman I'd been seeking all my life. She was clever, confident, and very beautiful, and until that moment her integrity was never in doubt.

'When you told me about what happened the night you were with Bevan's brother, and how you'd let Cassandra take the blame for what happened, I was sick because I'd put you on a pedestal, hadn't allowed for human error.'

'If anybody else had told me something like that I wouldn't have cared a damn, but I was like a silly kid who finds that his favourite toy isn't as marvellous as he'd thought, and though it's still brilliant he feels let down.

'I'd have forgotten the whole thing by the following day, but I knew all along that you wouldn't, and I've been miserably conscious that I blew it.'

'You made up for all that with the flowers and the note that was with them,' she said with a catch in her voice.' I couldn't get off the plane quickly enough. . .and here I am. I came straight from the airport.

'Let's go outside so that we don't waken Dad,' he said softly. 'He's doing fine, but he does need all the rest he can get.'

When they stood in the dimly lit corridor he said huskily, 'I meant what I said on the note, Lucinda,'

'That you'd no one to fill your stocking?' she teased.

'That, and the fact that I love you. I've wanted to tell you a dozen times, but there was always the thought at the back of my mind that maybe you really were looking forward to spending Christmas away from me. In the end I just had to risk it. . .and thank God I did!'

She giggled delightedly. 'Say that you love me again, Rafe' she murmured as she went into his outstretched arms. 'And just for the record. . .I love you, too, Rafe.'

'Do you? Do you really, Lucinda?' he said softly, and when she nodded solemnly with her eyes full of dreams he breathed, 'Show me!'

And she did, holding him to her as if she would never let him go, kissing him until she was breathless. Then he took over and it was like those other times, their bodies on fire, their hearts beating as one.

The second time she went to board the flight to Moscow it was January. Christmas and the New Year had gone and the coldest days of winter lay ahead, but Lucinda wasn't aware of the cold. This time Rafe was with her, holding her close as if he couldn't bear to let her out of his sight. And when it was time for them to separate she murmured against his lips, 'I'll be back in ten days, and then we'll be together for the rest of our lives. . .and Rafe?'

'What?' he asked tenderly.

'Thank you for the most wonderful Christmas of my life.'

He held her closer. 'But we didn't go anywhere. . .didn't do anything. . .except visit Dad, keep the kids company and cook the turkey.'

She nodded. 'Yes, that's right. . .and every moment was heaven. You have no idea how many glitzy Christmas times I've spent alone.'

'Not any more,' he assured her as the flight was called for a second time.

He looked down at the glowing ruby and diamond ring on her finger that they'd chosen as the shops were getting ready to close on Christmas Eve, and said in a low voice, 'When are we going to put a plain gold band next to the rubies?'

'Whenever you say,' she answered meekly with her dark eyes dancing.

'I love you when you're subservient, Lucinda,' he said as his arms tightened around her, 'and I love you even more when you're not.'

MILLS & BOON®

COLLECTOR'S EDITION

Look out next month for the Penny Jordan
Collector's Edition—a selection of her most popular stories,
published in beautifully designed volumes for you
to collect and cherish.

Starting with *You Owe Me* and *Lovers Touch* in June 1998,
there are two books every month for ten months, so
you can build your very own personal set of Penny's
finest romances.

On sale from 1st June from WH Smith, John Menzies,
Tesco, Asda, Martins Volume One and all good paperback
stockists at £3.10 each.

**Mail-in for free gifts
—see books for details**

4 FREE

books and a surprise gift!

We would like to take this opportunity to thank you for reading this Mills & Boon® book by offering you the chance to take FOUR more specially selected titles from the Medical Romance™ series absolutely FREE! We're also making this offer to introduce you to the benefits of the Reader Service™—

- ★ FREE home delivery
- ★ FREE gifts and competitions
- ★ FREE monthly newsletter
- ★ Books available before they're in the shops
- ★ Exclusive Reader Service discounts

Accepting these FREE books and gift places you under no obligation to buy, you may cancel at any time, even after receiving your free shipment. Simply complete your details below and return the entire page to the address below. *You don't even need a stamp!*

YES! Please send me 4 free Medical Romance books and a surprise gift. I understand that unless you hear from me, I will receive 4 superb new titles every month for just £2.30 each, postage and packing free. I am under no obligation to purchase any books and may cancel my subscription at any time. The free books and gift will be mine to keep in any case.

M8XE

Ms/Mrs/Miss/Mr ....Initials ....
BLOCK CAPITALS PLEASE

Surname ....

Address ....

....

....Postcode...................................

Send this whole page to:
THE READER SERVICE, FREEPOST, CROYDON, CR9 3WZ
(Eire readers please send coupon to: P.O. BOX 4546, DUBLIN 24.)

Offer not valid to current Reader Service subscribers to this series. We reserve the right to refuse an application and applicants must be aged 18 years or over. Only one application per household. Terms and prices subject to change without notice. Offer expires 30th November 1998. You may be mailed with offers from other reputable companies as a result of this application. If you would prefer not to receive such offers, please tick box. ☐

Medical Romance is being used as a trademark.